The Heart of Blackwood

A Briarvale Romance Novel

By Natalie G Ridley

1

Dedicated to my dear friend, Marina, who had been a source of constant joy, validation, and support.

Table Of Contents:

Chapter One – Page 4
Chapter Two – Page 13
Chapter Three – Page 21
Chapter Four – Page 30
Chapter Five – Page 39
Chapter Six – Page 48
Chapter Seven – Page 57
Chapter Eight – Page 69
Chapter Nine – Page 79
Chapter Ten – Page 88
Chapter Eleven – Page 97
Chapter Twelve – Page 110
Chapter Thirteen – Page 119
Chapter Fourteen – Page 131
Chapter Fifteen – Page 145
Chapter Sixteen – Page 156
Chapter Seventeen – Page 169
Chapter Eighteen – Page 181
Chapter Nineteen – Page 192
Chapter Twenty – Page 202
Chapter Twenty-One – Page 215

Chapter One

The wheels of the carriage clattered over the ancient stone road, each bump and creak amplified in the silence of the thickening mist. Through the small window, Isaac Blackwood watched the silhouette of Langston Manor slowly emerge, shrouded in fog like a spectre rising from the earth. Even after years away, the sight of the sprawling estate brought back the familiar weight of responsibility, a heaviness that pressed down on him like a stone upon his chest. He had never expected to return so soon – certainly not as the new Duke.

Isaac leaned back into his seat and exhaled slowly, his breath visible in the unseasonably cold summer air. The title of Duke Blackwood of Langston had been his father's until only a few weeks ago. Now it belonged to him, along with all the duties and expectations that came with it. He wasn't sure which was worse: inheriting the title or inheriting Langston Manor, a place that had never felt like home.

The Blackwood family had always been one of power and prestige in the kingdom of Briarvale, important enough that they had many lands which contributed to the successful harvest every year, as well as highly sought after salt and copper mines. But with their name came a shadow that stretched back for generations – a dark reputation that followed the family like a curse. Tragedies seemed to haunt the Blackwoods at every turn. Isaac had grown up hearing the whispered stories from the estate's staff, hushed conversations about the misfortunes that plagued the family: deaths, betrayals, madness, accidents. His own mother had died when he was only six, a sudden illness that no healer could explain and no tonic or elixir could alleviate. She was just one more name on a long list of losses that stretched back centuries.

His memories of her seemed to slip away more each time he tried to see her in his mind, her fair blonde hair, her upturned nose, and the way she'd hum to herself as she tatted lace were some of the few pieces that remained constant. The manor in which he'd lived for the most of his formative years never truly felt touched by her presence since her death. He'd heard the reverence many of the servants held for her, and the way some – such as the cook – continued many of the habits she'd cultivated in her short life. In a selfish way, he wondered if it had been for his benefit, their pity for the young boy he'd been when he'd lost her.

Though no one could say exactly where the tragedies began or why they occurred, the Blackwoods had long been rumoured to carry a curse. The staff spoke of it in veiled terms, and the people of Langston and the surrounding villages around the estate speculated endlessly. It was said that Blackwoods were destined for sorrow, doomed to suffer one misfortune after another. Isaac's father had believed in it, too – perhaps not openly at first, but in the way he had lived, always wary, always guarding against some unseen fate. He'd known the madness that so many other Blackwoods had dealt with, though Isaac was unsure on how deeply this gripped him in the end.

The carriage jolted as it turned into the estate, pulling Isaac from his thoughts. The towering oaks that lined the drive, stood like silent sentinels, their branches twisting overhead. The fog clung to the land, obscuring the horizon and giving the estate a dreamlike quality. Isaac felt a sense of foreboding as the manor loomed before him. Langston had always felt more like a mausoleum than a home – a place where joy and laughter were as absent as the warmth of the sun in winter.

The carriage came to a halt at the foot of the stone steps leading up to the grand entrance. Isaac sat for a moment longer, his hand resting on the door handle, reluctant to face what awaited him. His father had been such a distant figure in life, more a presence of duty than affection. Now, in death, the old Duke's expectations seemed even heavier. With a sigh, Isaac pushed the door open and stepped out into the mist.

The wind bit at him immediately, cold and sharp, rustling the dark cloak he had draped over his shoulders. Williams, the head butler and steward of Langston Manor, was waiting at the foot of the steps. His posture was as rigid and proper as Isaac remembered, his grey hair neatly combed, his expression one of quiet formality. The elder butler was more a constant in his formative life than even the governesses that came and went with the seasons it seemed. He must have greyed rather early in life, as Isaac had never known him to look any younger or indeed older.

"Your Grace," Williams said with a bow. "Welcome home."

Isaac gave a curt nod, unsure whether the word "home" could ever apply to this place. He had spent most of his childhood here, but he had never felt at ease within the manor's walls. It had always been cold, both physically and emotionally, a reflection of the man who had ruled it – his father.

His father had been a man of duty above all else. The most important thing he'd had the tutors and governesses impart onto him were the burdens of his title, even before etiquette and manners, it was always what a Blackwood had to stand for, and what a heavy burden they carried. His father had rarely been involved in his upbringing, retreating further into the isolated world of his study and estate business. Perhaps he had been afraid to grow close to Isaac, fearing that whatever had claimed his wife might one day claim his son.

The thought sent a familiar chill through Isaac. He had never truly understood the curse, but its effects had been clear enough. His mother's sudden death had been just one of the many tragedies that had scarred the Blackwood family. Others had suffered just as much, if not more. His uncle had drowned in a lake near the estate, his father's only sibling. His cousin, the only child of his uncle, had disappeared into the mountains of far off Destein, never to return. And yet, for all the sorrow that had surrounded his father, there had been one curious exception to the so-called curse.

Isaac's grandparents – his father's parents – had lived long and happy lives. They had loved each other deeply, and their union had been one of joy rather than duty. He'd known they'd caused some upset in the Kingdom when they'd married as he was aware that his grandmother should have been married to the second prince at the time, however she'd chosen his grandfather nevertheless. Isaac sometimes dared to believe that it was their love that shielded them from the frailties of the Blackwood blood, as nonsensical as that would seem. Though their own sons had been subject to the ill effects of it, so perhaps it was not as clear cut as that.

"Everything has been prepared for your return, Your Grace," Williams continued, his voice steady. "The staff is ready to assist you with anything you may need."

Isaac nodded again, his gaze sweeping over the assembled staff that stood outside the manor, each bowing as he passed. Most of the faces were familiar – people who had served his family for decades—but there were new ones as well, likely hired in his absence. He had spent the last several years in the capital, Acicularia, managing affairs on behalf of the estate from a distance, leaving the day-to-day running of Langston in his father's hands. Now, it was all his.

He deemed it important, at least, to know their names, for it was the least he'd be able to do for those that would serve him directly. He'd asked for Williams to supply him with a list for those he'd be unfamiliar with, brief physical descriptions, their duties. In all there weren't too many he had to learn, a new gamekeeper, some new scullery and kitchen maids, and near all of the stable-hands were new, and for the most part they were from the same families that had always served the Blackwoods.

As he climbed the wide stone steps, the door to Langston Manor creaked open, revealing the darkened interior. The entrance hall, with its vaulted ceiling and grand staircase, was much the same as he remembered it – vast and imposing, dominated by portraits of long-dead ancestors. Isaac glanced briefly at the rows of paintings, the faces of Blackwoods from generations past staring down at him with cold, unblinking eyes. They had all borne the weight of the family name, just as he would now. In his youth he tried to imagine that one day his own portrait would hang on the walls, and that his descendants would see somewhat of a different man in him.

Stepping inside, Isaac felt the familiar chill of the manor settle over him. The air was heavy with the scent of damp stone and aged wood, a smell that had never quite left the place despite the efforts of the servants to keep it clean. The fire in the great hearth at the far end of the hall offered little warmth, its flickering flames doing little to dispel the gloom.

"Your father's study remains as it was, Your Grace," Williams said from behind him. "Nothing has been disturbed."

Isaac's stomach tightened at the mention of his father's study. That room had always been the heart of Langston Manor – a place where decisions were made and where he was not allowed to step outside of learning what he'd one day come to inherit. His father had spent countless hours there, managing the estate, the town, and corresponding with the other noble families of Briarvale. It had been the old Duke's sanctuary, and now, it would become his. It felt wrong, as if he'd be slipping on a pair of his father's riding boots, yet it was always something he'd known would come to be some day.

"I'll see to it shortly," Isaac replied, his voice measured.

He ascended the grand staircase, his boots echoing softly against the polished wood of the steps. The corridor leading to his father's study was lined with more portraits, each figure depicted with the same stern expression that seemed to define the Blackwood line. They were all men and women who had lived under the shadow of the family's tragic history, each of them touched by loss in one way or another. Isaac had often wondered if the curse was real, or if it was simply the result of the Blackwood's unrelenting dedication to duty. After all, his grandparents had been spared much of the heartache. But why them, and why should his family be so inclined to suffering?

He reached the study door and hesitated for a moment before pushing it open. The room was just as he remembered it – dark, heavy with the scent of old leather and parchment, the large oak desk dominating the space. Papers lay scattered across its surface, ledgers and letters detailing the affairs of the estate, all left untouched since his father's passing.

Isaac stepped inside, closing the door softly behind him. The room felt like a time capsule, as though his father might walk in at any moment, ready to sit down and continue his endless work. But the silence was thick, and the fire in the hearth had long since died, leaving the room cold and lifeless.

Moving to the window, Isaac gazed out at the estate grounds, now obscured by the thickening mist. The lands of Langston stretched far beyond the manor – forests, fields, and rivers all under his rule now, the town itself could not be seen through the mists though he knew where it laid in relation to where he stood. It was beautiful, in a stark, desolate way, but Isaac felt no comfort in its vastness. The estate had always been more of a prison than a sanctuary.

He could still remember the stories the staff told in hushed tones, how they spoke of the Blackwood curse as though it were an undeniable truth. Tragedy had followed the family for centuries, and yet no one knew why. Some said it was the land itself, that the estate was built on cursed ground. Others claimed it was the Blackwood bloodline, tainted by some ancient sin. Whatever the cause, the tragedies were real enough, and Isaac could feel their weight as he stood there, staring out into the mist.

A soft knock at the door interrupted his thoughts.

"Your Grace," Williams called from the hall. "The staff awaits your instructions regarding the estate."

Isaac turned from the window, his expression hardening. "Of course," he said, his voice steady. He had a title to uphold and responsibilities to attend to. Langston Manor needed its Duke, curse or no curse.

But as he left the study, the weight of the Blackwood tragedies hung heavy in the air, like a whispered warning that he could not yet fully understand.

Chapter Two

The soft echo of hurried footsteps on polished stone floors was a familiar sound in Langston Manor, one that often went unnoticed amid the grandeur and quiet of the estate. For Amelda Gedge, however, each footfall felt louder than the last as she made her way down the dimly lit corridor, carrying a sealed letter in her hand. The flickering light of the wall sconces cast long shadows, and the faint chill of the strangely cold summer seeped through the old stone walls, making her cheeks flush slightly.

She'd not yet met the new Duke, as she'd been home with her family for a short leave for her sister's wedding when he'd arrived. He'd been reclusive in the study, and she'd only espied his figure briefly from afar in the gardens as she attended her duties, so she had no idea what sort of man he was. She'd asked some of the other staff, Mrs Henderson, Clara, Williams – what they made of the man. The cook said he was simply a young man getting used to his newfound title. Her fellow maid said that he looked dashing, and had kind, albeit, sad eyes so she reckoned he was still in mourning. The butler had told her he was an educated man, and a good man – though did not explain anything further.

She was used to the quietness, the stillness of the manor that seemed to settle in like dust on old furniture. Amelda had been working at Langston Estate for just over three years, but in that time, she had become adept at going unnoticed. It was a skill every servant at the estate learned – how to blend into the background, to move like shadows so as not to disturb the lives of the nobility they served. It was how the late Duke preferred things to be and Amelda was particularly good at it.

She was like her mother, tall and slender, with dark red hair that, in most lights, could easily be mistaken for brown, and had the kind of presence that could fade into the surroundings of Langston's grand halls and towering ceilings. Her face, lightly freckled from her days working in the gardens before being moved to the manor and a childhood playing in the fields around her village was ordinary insofar as she was concerned, and the freckles reminded her of her late father as he'd been covered in the small brown marks. The flush in her cheeks – whether from exertion or the crisp air – gave her a healthy glow that contrasted with the muted colours of the uniform she wore.

Amelda felt set apart from many of the other staff in the manor, as she hadn't come from any of the families that prided themselves in being in service to the Blackwoods. She had grown up in a small village not far from the estate, her father a blacksmith and her mother a seamstress. Life had been simple but full of warmth until her father's untimely death – an accident at the forge. With her family's financial situation becoming precarious, Amelda had sought work at Langston Estate, at least until she would be married, though she felt no rush. She had started in the garden, then the kitchens, later promoted to work in the manor itself, where the duties were more refined, the expectations higher.

She still was tasked with jobs in the garden or kitchen at times, when someone was unwell or on leave, so for the most part she felt between spaces.

Tonight, her task was simple. She had been given the letter by Mrs. Fletcher, the head housekeeper, and instructed to deliver it directly to the new Duke – Isaac Blackwood. Amelda knew of him in an abstract way, the long-awaited son who had inherited the title after the former Duke's passing. He had been away for years before she'd joined the staff. He'd been studying in the capital, and managing far reaching matters of the family from afar, and his presence in Langston Manor was still the subject of quiet curiosity amongst the servants that had come to join the staff in that absence. Amelda had never seen him up close, though she knew of him, as all the servants did. The Blackwood name was one spoken with reverence and a hint of fear in the village she'd grown up in, and from her time under the late Duke, she'd understood why. The tragedies that followed the family were well-known, and she'd heard stories of a mystical curse. Whether she actually believed it was a curse or a tale for children so they'd learn to behave was something she'd yet to decide.

Reaching the large oak door that led to the study, Amelda paused. She had never entered the Duke's study before, and the thought of intruding on such a private space filled her with a sudden sense of unease. The study had always been the domain of the former Duke, a place of quiet authority where important matters of the estate were discussed and decided. Even when she had delivered messages or letters in the past, she had never been asked to step inside and the door had only ever been cracked enough to allow the letter to pass the threshold.

Her fingers hovered over the door for a moment before she rapped softly, her knock barely audible in the vastness of the corridor.

"Enter," came a voice from within.

Amelda hesitated briefly, then pushed the door open, stepping into the dimly lit room. The study was just as imposing as she had imagined, with towering bookshelves that stretched to the ceiling, their shelves crammed with leather-bound volumes. The fireplace along the far wall cast a warm but subdued glow over the space, though it did little to lift the sense of cold that seemed to cling to the room. The whole manor was cold, even in the height of summer – which was a blessed relief when she'd worked in the gardens, but there was something entirely different about the cold in the study.

Behind the large oak desk, Isaac Blackwood sat, his eyes fixed on the papers before him. He looked up as she entered, his expression unreadable. The new Duke was younger than Amelda had imagined, though the weight of his title already seemed to have settled on his shoulders. His face was sharp, with a chiselled jaw and an intensity in his gaze that she found difficult to meet directly. His dark hair, neatly trimmed, fell just slightly over his brow, casting a shadow over his grey eyes.

"Your Grace," she said quietly, keeping her voice steady as she stepped forward. "A letter for you."

Isaac's gaze shifted from the letter in her hand to her face, and for the first time, Amelda felt his eyes really take her in. She had expected him to glance briefly at her before returning to his work, as so many others of his status often did with servants. But instead, there was a moment – just a flicker – where his attention lingered on her longer than it should have. It was subtle, almost imperceptible, but enough to make Amelda's heart race. It was as if he was looking at her, and weighing everything he could see – not in a cruel way, but certainly with more inspection than she was used to from anyone.

He took the letter from her hand without a word at first, his fingers brushing hers briefly. The touch was fleeting, but it left her more aware of the space between them, and of the quiet in the room. It was in that breath she could see in him some dreadful, desperate loneliness which made her ache.

"Thank you," Isaac said, his voice low and formal.

Amelda quickly dropped her gaze, suddenly conscious of her own presence in the room. She had always prided herself on her ability to remain invisible, to pass unnoticed in the halls of Langston Manor. But here, under the Duke's gaze, she felt uncomfortably seen, and likewise felt like a voyeur who had seen too much.

"Is there anything else, Your Grace?" she asked, her voice soft.

Isaac didn't answer immediately, still studying her with a curiosity that seemed out of place. He was a man accustomed to control, that much was clear from the way he held himself, but there was something in his expression that suggested a momentary lapse – a flicker of something he hadn't quite expected.

"No," he finally replied. "That will be all."

Amelda nodded and turned to leave, moving quickly towards the door, eager to escape the room and the strange tension that seemed to hang in the air. She could feel Isaac's gaze on her as she moved, and it made her acutely aware of her every step, every movement. She hadn't expected him to notice her, let alone to look at her with such intent.

The door closed softly behind her, and Amelda let out a breath she hadn't realised she'd been holding. She stood in the corridor for a moment, steadying herself, before making her way back towards the servants' quarters. The encounter had been brief, nothing more than a simple delivery, and yet it had left her unsettled. Clara had been accurate in that he'd seemed sad, though the enormity of that feeling didn't truly match the word as her fellow maid described it.

As she hurried down the stairs and through the narrow corridors that led to the heart of the manor's working quarters, Amelda's mind raced. She had always kept her head down, avoided drawing attention to herself. The hierarchy of Langston was rigid, and there were clear lines between the servants and the family they served. Yet something compelled her to close that chasm and balm the sadness she'd seen etched on his face.

And the Duke had looked at her – really looked at her. And in that brief moment, something had passed between them, though she couldn't quite name what it was. She had seen many visiting nobles in her time at Langston, most of them distant and preoccupied with their own affairs. But Isaac Blackwood had been different. There had been an intensity in his gaze, something deeper than the casual indifference she had expected.

By the time she reached the small kitchen that served as the servants' retreat, Amelda had managed to push the strange encounter from her mind. There was still work to be done – fireplaces to be stoked, linens to be folded, and rooms to be prepared for the following day. Whatever had happened in the Duke's study was surely just a passing moment, nothing more. She put it down to curiosity and some tiredness, trying to put the unsettled feeling out of her mind.

But as she busied herself with her duties, her fingers working mechanically, her mind kept drifting back to that room – the warmth of the firelight, the coldness of the air, and the dark eyes of Isaac Blackwood watching her with a quiet, unreadable intensity.

Isaac sat back in his chair after she had left, the letter forgotten in his hand. He wasn't sure what had just happened, but it had stirred something in him. The maid,

Amelda, was it? Hadn't been what he had expected. She hadn't been here the day he'd arrived. There was something about her that had drawn his attention in a way he hadn't anticipated.

It was unusual for him to notice the servants at all, they were particularly quiet even for his experiences of servants elsewhere. They were part of the fabric of Langston Manor, performing their duties quietly and efficiently, blending into the background as they were trained to do. But Amelda had disrupted that quiet, unobtrusive flow, if only for a moment. He couldn't quite place what it was – perhaps the way her dark red hair had caught the firelight, or the way her cheeks were flushed with the cool evening air, he'd even caught a faint scent of something floral about her that he couldn't quite place – but whatever it was, it had left him unsettled.

He turned the letter over in his hand, his mind still distracted. It was a likely some trivial matter – estate business that could wait until morning. For now, he let his gaze linger on the door through which Amelda had exited, the faint echoes of her footsteps fading down the corridor.

Something had shifted in Langston Manor tonight, and Isaac couldn't help but wonder what it might mean.

Chapter Three

Isaac sat alone in his study, despite the cool of the morning air penetrating the walls he would have sworn he felt something warmer, like an unnamed presence that was reaching for him. The fire crackled softly, casting a gentle glow that flickered across the walls, illuminating the dark oak of the bookshelves. Yet, despite the warmth of the flames and whatever else he was sure he was imagining, an oppressive chill settled in Isaac's chest, the burdens of his title pressing down upon him like an anchor.

He turned his attention back to the letter he'd left abandoned. The envelope was unremarkable, a simple piece of parchment sealed with wax. Carefully, he broke the seal and unfolded the letter, revealing two letters in fact. In the first, the familiar handwriting of his father's lawyer unfurled before him. As he began to read, the room fell silent, the crackling fire the only sound in the vast space.

To His Grace, Isaac Blackwood, Duke of Langston,

I extend my sincere condolences on the passing of your father. Augustus Blackwood was a man of complexity and depth, whose legacy is now in your hands. As per his last wishes, I have the solemn duty of delivering this letter to you upon your assumption of the title of Duke.

My Dearest Isaac,

If you are reading this, it means I have succumbed to the weight of my own burdens and have departed from this world. I wish I could say that my absence will not affect you, but you and I both know the truth: our lives have long been intertwined with the shadows of our family name.

You inherit not only the title of Duke but the spectres that haunt the Blackwood blood. You have heard the whispers, I am sure. Those born of our blood, and indeed even those who have married us, seem doomed to endure a series of misfortunes that would crush the spirit of a stronger soul than yours or mine.

In truth, I have struggled to provide you with the affection you deserved, and it pains me to even write such a thing, though I hope to be forgiven in this next life. My own troubles and despair often kept me distant, preoccupied with fears that held me captive. While I married your mother as a much younger man, full of vigour and some might say hope, it was not long after our arrangement came to pass that the curse reared it's head. A series of accidents occurred that nearly took both of our lives. I searched for answered for years, biding my time in having any heirs that I might not foist such a burden onto them – as it stands of course, you came to arrive regardless of any intents to wait for a cure to this curse. I considered you a blessing, and still do, but such a blessing that I dared not waver from looking for answers. I did not find much, and what I did collate, you will find in the library if you wish to continue the search. I fear that I have unwittingly passed my own torments onto you. For that, I hope you can forgive me as much as my maker might.

Take heed of my warnings: should you choose to marry, do so with great caution. The darkness that enveloped your mother in her final days serves as a grim reminder of the perils that lurk in love and affection. Limit your heart's reach, for to love deeply is to invite suffering. I could not protect your mother, and I fear I cannot protect you either. It was perhaps luck that we did not marry for love, for her loss might have cut an even deeper wound in my heart.

Yet, even as I write these words, a small part of me yearns for you to know a different kind of love – one that is unencumbered by the constraints of duty or fear. I often find myself regretting the path I chose, the distance I kept, and the moments of joy I let slip away.

I cannot change the past, and I cannot alter the course of your life. But as you step into this role, I ask you to consider your own heart and what it could endure should the curse affect you. The burdens of our title can be heavy, and the expectations overwhelming, but you have the power to carve your own path.

Remember that, even in my absence, you are not alone. I may have struggled to show you, but I carry a hope for you in my heart. May you navigate this world with both strength and grace, even as you bear the weight of our name.

With a father's regret,
Augustus Blackwood

Isaac felt as though the air had been sucked from the room. The words swirled around him like leaves in a tempest, each phrase a reminder of the heavy mantle he had inherited, and the thickness of the blood in his veins. His father's warnings echoed in his mind – do not feel too deeply, marry quickly, remain aloof. It was a dire blueprint for a life he had never wanted.

Even with such grim advice, it was more lucid and warm than anything he'd known his father to have been.

He sank back into his chair, the letter trembling slightly in his hands as the shadows of the past threatened to engulf him. The loss of his mother had been a spectre that loomed large over his childhood, an empty seat at the table that was never filled. Her absence had been an aching silence in a household already steeped in distance and duty. Isaac's father had loved her in his own way, that much he had come to understand over the years, but that love had not saved her from the curse that had come to claim its due.

Isaac had often wondered if his father had believed in the curse or if it was merely a tale spun to placate the fears of a young boy. His grandparents had never acknowledged the curse from what he remembered of them; they were carefree and mirthful despite the duties of managing Langston and it's surrounding environs. They had lived long lives, well

into their twilight years, surrounded by laughter and joy –
untouched by the tragedy that had befallen the Blackwood
line before or since. Perhaps that had been the key: to put
the curse out of his mind, to pretend it did not exist.

But the warnings were unmistakable. Isaac could almost
hear his father's stern voice, a man hardened by the burden
of duty, telling him to approach his affairs with caution.
Yet, the thought of marrying for obligation alone filled him
with dread. The mere thought of having to share his life
with someone who was more stranger than lover so as to not
mourn their loss if, or indeed when, his curse would touch
them sounded like divine punishment.

His fingers tightened around the edges of the letter, his
thoughts drifting to the vibrant life he had led in the capital
before his father's death. The lectures at the university had
sparked a flame within him, igniting his passion for
philosophy and history. He had attended soirées where the
air was thick with laughter and music, and his peers had
engaged in spirited debates over glasses of fine wine. Those
days had felt alive with possibility, free from the weight of
expectation that now clung to him like a shroud.

Now, standing in this vast, sombre manor, he was tethered
to the past, haunted by the ghosts of what had been and
what could never be. The responsibilities of his title felt like
chains, binding him to the estate and its unyielding
traditions. He closed his eyes, leaning back in the chair as
the fire crackled softly beside him, casting flickering
shadows across the room. He yearned for a life that was

vibrant and unrestrained, one that didn't revolve around duty and obligation.

There was a knock at the door, pulling Isaac from his reverie. He straightened, smoothing the letter against the desk before calling, "Enter."

The door creaked open, and in walked Williams, he exuded an air of competence and calm he felt almost jealous of. He was a fixture at Langston Manor, a steadying force who had guided the estate through the years of his father's stern hand.

"Your Grace," Williams said, inclining his head respectfully. "I trust you've had time to settle in?"

"Thank you, Williams," Isaac replied, forcing a semblance of warmth into his tone. "I have, indeed. I was just reviewing some correspondence."

"Of course." Williams's sharp eyes glanced at the letter on the desk before returning to Isaac's face. "There are several matters that require your attention. The estate's finances need to be reviewed, and I believe the harvest this year has been quite bountiful. We should consider the best course of action for selling the surplus."

Isaac nodded, mentally shifting gears. The practicalities of the estate were a welcome distraction from the weight of the letter and the burden of his title. "Yes, let's discuss that. I'm also aware of the state of the tenants. Have any issues arisen since my return?"

"Nothing pressing, Your Grace. The farmers have all been compliant with their dues. However, there have been whispers of discontent among some of the labourers. They believe the harvest might yield more than previously agreed, and they seek fair compensation."

"Then we must address it," Isaac said, he'd been groomed for these duties all his life, and at the very least he'd be a decent steward to the people to whom he'd been entrusted. "Our tenants deserve to be heard. Schedule a meeting with them for next week. I want to speak with them directly."

Williams regarded him with a nod of approval, the faintest hint of a smile playing at the corners of his mouth. "Very well, Your Grace. I will arrange it."

"Thank you," Isaac said, relieved to shift the focus away from his own troubles. The affairs of the estate, while heavy in their own right, allowed him a modicum of control over his life. He could shape the world around him, rather than remain a passive player trapped by the chains of his title.

As they continued to discuss the matters of Langston, Isaac felt the burdens of the Blackwood legacy ease, if only for a moment. The weight of his father's warnings still loomed over him, but with each decision he made for the estate, he found a flicker of hope – the hope that he could forge a new path, one not entirely dictated by the shadows of the past.

Yet, even as he immersed himself in the duties of a Duke, Isaac's thoughts wandered back to the maid. He'd checked over his notes from Williams about all the new staff and was certain that she must be Amelda Gedge. The fleeting moments of their encounter played through his mind, her flushed cheeks and that brief touch of her warm fingers against his own as she'd passed him the letter. It unsettled and excited him at once in a way he'd been quite unprepared for. There had been something in her gaze that resonated with him, like she'd seen more of him than his title, peeked at his soul and something that stirred feelings he had long since buried beneath the weight of expectation. He would have felt less keenly observed stripped bare for a physician than he'd done in that moment with her.

Perhaps it was foolish to dwell on a mere maid, someone he'd likely see in passing often enough that they'd become as familiar as the portraits or the paths in the garden, yet he couldn't help but wonder about her story. Did she, too, feel the chains of duty as he did? Or had she carved a life for herself amidst the confines of the manor, her heart unburdened by the responsibilities that he felt so keenly? Who was she to even occupy his thoughts this much?

That evening, after Williams had departed, Isaac found himself back in the study, the fire crackling softly. He stared out at the darkening sky, the shadows deepening in the corners of the room. The letter lay on the desk, its warnings still fresh in his mind, but for the first time, he felt a glimmer of rebellion against its stifling message.

Could he actually break the curse, if it even existed? Coincidences, tragic as they were, would explain things neatly. He could act as his grandparents did and act on as if nothing cruel could befall them. Was it that they even dared to grasp for happiness the reason they ever achieved any?

As the night deepened and the stars began to twinkle outside the window, Isaac made a silent vow to himself: he would seek the truth of the matter, it had claimed too many to feel like coincidence, and was targeted on the Blackwood name. It was either a foul magic that he would solve, or the dangers of believing in myths that poisoned his bloodline. Either way, he would not be a slave to half-truths nor magic.

He stood up, the embers of the fire glowing warmly in the hearth, and turned to the door. Whatever awaited him in the days to come, he would face it with the same resolve he had felt in the capital. The shadows of the past would not dictate his future; he would carve his own path through the darkness.

And perhaps, just perhaps, there was light to be found in the most unexpected of places.

Chapter Four

Amelda's days at Langston Estate were often punctuated by the rhythm of routine ironing linens, polishing the silverware, and preparing meals in the vast kitchens under Mrs Henderson or tending to the gardens should Mrs Fletcher not be in need of her. Yet, in the quiet moments stolen from her duties, when the house settled into its evening stillness, she found solace in her secret passion: reading. The world beyond the estate's imposing walls was a vast tapestry of stories and great minds full of radical ideas waiting to be woven into her mind, and nowhere was that tapestry richer than in the manor's library.

The late Duke had frequented the room only in the mornings, when he was most lucid, sequestering himself by the afternoons, and it seemed the new Duke had yet to take in the magnificence of the library. She supposed he was either too busy, or perhaps he was not an avid reader.

The library was a sanctuary for Amelda, a hidden alcove where the scent of old parchment and leather-bound volumes mingled with the faint aroma of polished wood. It was a place where the echoes of history whispered through the pages of the books, inviting her to lose herself in tales of distant lands and bygone eras. Her favourite tales and reference books often had pictures in them too – exotic birds from far off kingdoms she'd never get to see outside of the pages. They were astounding, and she was jealous of those who could call such beasts commonplace. She hoped that they too were jealous of her being able to glimpse at the native creatures of Briarvale where they'd never seen such beauties, which comforted her in a way.

On this particular evening, as the sun dipped below the horizon, casting long shadows across the room, Amelda slipped away from her duties and into the comforting embrace of the library.

She had always been drawn to books – whether they were grand tales of heroic knights or fables of lost love, even the non-fiction was exciting. As a child, she would gather around the fire with her siblings, listening intently to her father's tales of the folk of Briarvale, those who danced with faeries under the moonlight or challenged dragons atop distant mountains. Then, as she grew older her sister would bring back books from the village library, and later, share her gifts from her now husband that he'd send to her while they were courting. Each story ignited her imagination, kindling a longing for adventure that was often stifled by the constraints of her daily life.

As Amelda entered the library, she closed the heavy oak door behind her, ensuring the outside world remained at bay. The room was illuminated by the dying light of the day, its warm glow highlighting the rows of books that towered like ancient sentinels. Dust motes danced in the air, swirling around her as she moved further into the room, her fingers grazing the spines of the volumes with reverent curiosity.

She wandered over to a grand wooden table, its surface cluttered with scrolls and manuscripts that had clearly not been touched in some time. Among them, one particular book caught her eye – a large tome bound in rich burgundy leather, its gilded title gleaming even in the dim light: Legends of Briarvale: The Myths and Folklore of the Blackwood Line.

Amelda's heart quickened as she picked it up, its weight both reassuring and foreboding. She settled into a nearby armchair, its fabric worn but inviting, and opened the book with a soft crackle of aged pages. The smell of old paper wafted up to her, a scent she had come to associate with adventure and knowledge.

As she began to read, Amelda found herself entranced by the tales of the Blackwood family – stories of bravery, sorrow, and the inexplicable connections that bound them to the land of Briarvale. The legends spoke of their forebears, noble figures who had carved their names into the annals of history, but amidst the accounts of valour, there were also hints of a darkness that shadowed the family line.

A chapter titled The Blackwood Curse beckoned to her, and Amelda's fingers traced the words as she read on, her curiosity piqued.

The legend speaks of a curse that befell the Blackwood family long ago, a punishment for their ancestors' choices. It is said that those of this bloodline are doomed to endure tragedies and misfortunes, a cruel inheritance that haunts their lives. The first Duke of Blackwood, in his pursuit of wealth and status, is believed to have made a bargain that ultimately sealed the fate of his descendants.

It is whispered that the curse takes many forms – loss of loved ones, an unholy madness, and an uncanny series of unfortunate events. Those who bear the Blackwood name seem to attract calamity, often encountering obstacles that thwart their deepest desires. The fate of each Duke, it seems, is tethered to this lingering shadow.

Some say the origins of the curse can be traced back to an ancient ritual conducted by the first Duke. In his ambition, he sought to bind his family's fortune to the land, offering a sacrifice to gain prosperity. However, the spirits of Briarvale, offended by this act of hubris, enacted a retribution that would plague the Blackwoods for generations. Others speculate that the curse was born from jealousy, a vengeful spirit seeking to punish those who rose above their station.

Amelda's breath hitched as she absorbed the words. The notion of a curse tied to choices made by long-dead ancestors felt both tragic and cruel, stirring something deep within her. It felt out of a fable from her childhood, some lesson in morality that was obscured by a hideous monster that devoured unkind princes and princesses or kindly magician who bestowed gifts unto good children who aided lost travellers.

As she continued to read, she learned of various Blackwood ancestors from long before her lifetime, their lives each punctuated by heartache. There was Lady Eliza, who expanded the territories of Langston in a vicious war, ending that war with a marriage with one of the sons from a neighbouring county, only to lose him to a tragic accident on the very eve of their wedding anniversary a year later. The narrative spoke of the pain in her heart, a loss that was said to have aged her rapidly. Another tale recounted the story of Duke Frederick, whose arranged marriage brought him great wealth but left him hollow and seeking companionship at every quarter. While he revolutionised the town at the time, and added to the estate a grand new wing, he was never satisfied with anything. He wandered the estate, haunted by the love he had never known, until he ultimately succumbed to despair having never found any.

Her eyebrows shot up in surprise, as Mrs Fletcher, sensible as she was, would speak of this ghostly apparition in the East Wing that made her so unbearably sad that she couldn't bear more than an hour in those rooms. Amelda wondered if the two were somehow related, though given if it was real and not the head housekeeper preferring to remain in the warmer parts of the estate she had no idea how she'd seek to mend the heart of a ghost that would have been dead over two hundred years.

Amelda's mind raced, the weight of the stories settling upon her like a heavy cloak. These were not mere tales of fiction; they were the echoes of a family ravaged by tragedy and heartache most cruel, some even leaned into what felt like torture. Her fingers lingered on the page as she absorbed each detail, her heart heavy with empathy for those who had suffered.

Yet, it was not only sorrow that filled her heart; it was also an abiding curiosity about the new Duke himself. Isaac Blackwood, she recalled, had looked upon her with a glance that felt like the first brush of sunlight after a long winter. He was a man shaped by loss, a man who had grown up for the most of his life without his mother and now bore the heavy burden of his father's passing. Amelda had seen the shadows beneath his eyes, the weight of expectation that hung upon his shoulders like a rain-cloud.

What had he truly felt upon learning of his father's death? How did it feel to grow up in a home filled with duty and obligation rather than love and warmth? The notion of his sorrow lingered in her thoughts, mingling with her intrigue. Unlike the visiting nobles, who often swept past her without a second glance, Isaac had taken notice. In their brief encounter, his gaze had met hers with a breathtaking scrutiny that occupied her mind even now. That simple recognition had ignited something within her, a flicker of hope that perhaps, beneath the weight of titles and expectations, he might also be searching for understanding.

Amelda's musings were interrupted by the sound of footsteps approaching the library. Panic coursed through her, and she quickly closed the book, returning it to the table just as the door swung open.

"Amelda," came a familiar voice, smooth and low. It was Mr Williams, the head butler, his expression one of mild surprise. "What are you doing in here?"

"I – um," Amelda stammered, her cheeks flushing as she attempted to gather her composure. "I was just... dusting the books."

Williams raised an eyebrow, his gaze flicking over the table cluttered with books and scrolls. "It appears that you've become rather engrossed in your work. This is quite a collection, is it not?"

"Yes, sir," she replied, her heart racing as she fought to appear nonchalant. "I find it all quite fascinating."

"Indeed," Williams nodded, a faint smile appearing at the corners of his mouth. He glanced at the book she'd been so engrossed in then back at her. "The Blackwood family history is filled with both remarkable triumphs and unfortunate tragedies. Few tales are without their darkness."

Amelda felt a chill creep down her spine, a reminder of the weight of the supposed curse that hung over the Blackwoods. "Do you believe in the curse?" she asked, surprising even herself with the boldness of her question.

Williams paused, his expression shifting as he considered her words. "It is easy to dismiss such things as mere superstition," he said slowly. He sucked in a deep breath. "But there is something to be said for the power of belief. Many in the town and even amongst the staff speak of it as a tangible thing, and that holds greater weight than you or I could fathom."

"So the belief itself can be dangerous," Amelda murmured, her thoughts lingering on the tales she had just read.

"Indeed," he replied, a thoughtful look crossing his face. "But sometimes, those beliefs can lead us to truths we may not want to face."

The moment hung between them, charged with an unspoken understanding. Amelda felt a sudden kinship with Williams, a shared awareness of the shadows that loomed over Langston Estate. While he was many years her senior, he had such an air of wisdom about him that felt fatherly. Her heart ached for her own father, and she smiled sadly.

"Thank you for indulging my curiosity, sir," Amelda said, her voice steadying. "I must return to my duties now."

"Of course," Williams said, his tone returning to its customary professionalism. "I will leave you to it. But remember, Amelda, knowledge is power. The more you understand the world around you, the better equipped you will be to face it."

With that, he departed, leaving Amelda alone once more in the hushed sanctuary of the library. As the door closed behind him, she returned to her seat and stared at the book, its spine shimmering under the flickering candlelight.

The words within had awakened something in her, a desire to unravel the threads of fate that bound the Blackwoods. She wanted to know the stories that remained unspoken. Which parts were fictional and cautionary and the parts that were truly part of the fabric which made up the household and family she served.

She slipped the book into her apron so that she could continue to read it tonight by the candlelight of her bed. She ought to return to dusting and not indulging her want for knowledge.

That night, as she turned the pages, the darkness of the estate faded into the background, and the flickering candlelight illuminated a path toward discovery. She was more than just a maid in Langston Estate; she was a seeker of stories, a weaver of dreams, and perhaps, in time, her imagination lead her to think of a time where she'd uncover some mystical relic secreted away in a dark corner that was the true reason behind this Blackwood Curse.

Chapter Five

The morning sun filtered through the dense canopy of trees
that surrounded the gardens of Langston Estate, casting
dappled patterns of light and shadow upon the manicured
lawns. The Duke, Isaac Blackwood strolled along the
cobbled path, his thoughts heavy with the burdens of his
newly inherited title. There was so much work to be done,
far more than his duties had entailed as merely the heir to
the duchy and he wondered if it was not just the fear of
some curse but the stresses that had given rise to the ills that
had staked his family line. The garden was a calm escape
from the oppressive atmosphere of the manor, yet even here,
the spectre of isolation loomed as much as the ever present
mist.

Isaac paused beside a cluster of blooming roses, their
vibrant colours a sharp contrast to the muted tones of his
world. He inhaled deeply, taking in their sweet fragrance, a
brief reprieve from the haunting memories of he had of
growing up here. The estate felt eerily quiet this morning,
more so than usual. It was as if it too were mourning the
loss of the man who had ruled over it.

He often found himself yearning for the camaraderie of his friends back in Acicularia – he'd yet to invite anyone during the official mourning period, and wished for a few more of those carefree days filled with scholarly debates and laughter. Now, as Duke, he was acutely aware of the expectations that accompanied his position. Duty governed his life, dictating every choice and restricting every impulse. Then of course there were the traditions that needed to be upheld beyond that. Naming an heir until he could marry and make one – it would likely be his distant cousin Theodore given how pruned his family tree was. And of course the matter of marriage itself. Somehow within the year he'd have to find a bride which could tolerate living here in Langston, as well as someone who would be tolerable for him to live alongside. There was little room for romance or warmth, it felt more like any other business dealing he had to sign for and the solitude felt more pronounced with each passing day.

Just as he was about to turn back towards the manor, a figure caught his eye. Amelda Gedge, the maid who had crossed his path just days before, was emerging from the back of the gardens, from the personal fields where the crops used in the manor were grown. She carried with a her basket filled with fresh produce. The bright colours of the vegetables seemed to bring her to life against the dull backdrop of the estate, and he couldn't help but watch as she approached the herb garden.

Amelda's dark red hair caught the sunlight, framing her face in a halo that made her look almost ethereal. As she moved, there was a gracefulness to her that caught his breath in his throat. Isaac had never been one to notice such things about the fairer sex, and there had been plenty of women in the capital who'd been famed for their beauty, who dressed extravagantly, yet there was something about her that stirred a curiosity within him. Perhaps it was the way she seemed to be a part of the shadows of the manor, yet somehow stood apart from them.

"Good morning, Amelda," Isaac called out, surprising himself with the nervous excitement in his tone.

She looked up, her cheeks flushing slightly as she met his gaze. "Good morning, Your Grace," she replied, her voice steady despite the surprise evident in her wide eyes.

"What are you carrying there?" he asked, nodding toward the basket in her arms.

"Oh, just some fresh vegetables for the kitchen," she said, her gaze flickering to the ground as she adjusted her hold on the basket. "Courgettes, rhubarb, radishes, gooseberries, cabbage, and some chicory – oh you don't need me to go on. Mrs Henderson likes everything brought in promptly so she can start the menu on time."

"May I offer my assistance?" Isaac gestured towards the basket, half-expecting her to accept. It felt almost ridiculous to think that he, Duke Blackwood, would be helping a servant with her duties, but the impulse to connect with her was undeniable.

Amelda hesitated, her brow furrowing slightly. "Oh, no, Your Grace, I couldn't possibly allow that," she said, a hint of concern creeping into her voice. "The cook would think it improper and accuse me of being lazy. I must do this myself."

"Surely she wouldn't mind," he pressed, attempting to inject a bit of levity into the moment. He knew enough of the cook that she'd served the family his entire life, and had a sweet spot for him as a child as she'd supplied him with sweetmeats and tarts aplenty. "I can assure you, I'm quite strong enough to carry a few vegetables."

She gave a soft laugh, the sound like a ripple of water in the stillness of the garden. "It's not about strength, Your Grace. It's about appearances. I wouldn't want to give her cause to think I'm neglecting my duties."

Isaac frowned, a sense of frustration bubbling beneath the surface. It was as if some inner force within him needed to just be in this woman's presence, if only a moment. "But you shouldn't have to bear the burden alone. There's no shame in asking for help."

Amelda met his gaze, and for a moment, the world around them faded. There was a shared understanding in her eyes, it was as if there was an acknowledgment of the burdens they both carried, and while he knew little more than her name he sensed some kindred spirit in that she bore a weight within her from duty just as he did. "Thank you for your kindness, but I assure you, I am quite capable," she replied, her tone firm yet respectful.

Isaac studied her for a moment, intrigued by the determination that shone through her gentle demeanour. There was a strength in her that resonated with him, a quiet resolve that spoke volumes. "Very well," he said at last, a small smile creeping onto his lips. "But I do hope you know you can ask for help if you ever need it."

"I appreciate that, Your Grace," she replied, a hint of warmth returning to her voice. "But for now, I shall manage. Besides, I'd rather not the gossip that would come from having the Duke seen polishing bannisters or cleaning the flue."

They stood in silence for a moment, the air thick with an unspoken connection that neither of them fully understood. The garden, once a simple backdrop to their conversation, had transformed into a sanctuary where the burdens of solitude and the chasm between their stations in life felt a little less heavy, a little less distant.

"How are you finding the position here at Langston?" Isaac ventured, his curiosity getting the better of him. "I noted when I arrived you had only been here three years or so."

Amelda glanced down at the basket, her fingers absently smoothing the fabric around the handle. "It is... different," she admitted. "But as you said, it's been just a bit over three years now, so it feels familiar in a way. I just try to do my best, as any servant would."

Isaac nodded, contemplating her words. "I suppose we all must do our best in the roles we are given," he said thoughtfully. "Though it often feels like our choices are limited."

Amelda's gaze met his, and a flicker of understanding passed between them. "That is true," she said quietly. "But sometimes, within those limitations, there is still room for… exploration."

"Exploration?" Isaac echoed, intrigued. He felt his pulse quicken under his collar.

"Yes, exploration of knowledge, of the self. Even within the confines of lives, we can find little moments of freedom." She smiled softly.

Isaac considered her words, his mind racing, he had been taken aback but was thrilled nevertheless. There was a depth to her that he had not expected, and he was delighted by it.

"And what do you seek to explore, Amelda?" he asked, genuinely curious.

Her eyes brightened, and for a brief moment, her shyness seemed to melt away. "I have always been fascinated by the legends of Briarvale," she confessed. "History, natural sciences, philosophy, and I have a weakness for stories. There's this joy I find when story and reality intertwine."

Isaac felt a swell of admiration for her passion. "I can understand the allure of stories. They have a way of connecting us to the past, don't they? They remind us that we are not alone, that others have walked similar paths."

"Yes," she agreed, her expression thoughtful. "And in understanding the past, we can perhaps shape our own future."

There was a moment of silence between them, each lost in their own thoughts. Isaac found himself contemplating what she had said, how it applied to his own runaway thoughts, and how in seeking to understand his lineage, perhaps there was a way to break free from the constraints of his title, or curse as the case might be.

"I have often felt that way," he admitted, breaking the stillness. "Though I fear I am bound by my duties."

"You are not alone in feeling that way, Your Grace," she replied gently. She jostled the basket carefully, tightening her grip on the handle. "We all have our own responsibilities, our own expectations. It can feel isolating and immensely stressful at times."

"Indeed," he said, there was a lot of truth in her words that he felt keenly. "Yet, perhaps there is a way to find connection, even in that isolation."

Amelda smiled at him, and in that moment, Isaac felt a flicker of hope. Maybe their meeting had not been a coincidence, but rather a gentle nudge from fate. Her ability to somehow see the crux of his issues and balm at those with an understanding he'd not anticipated made him feel all the more strongly that he would seek to steal more moments of her time when their paths should cross again. He'd relish it.

"Thank you for indulging my curiosity, Amelda," Isaac said, grateful for the brief glimpse into a world that felt so distant from his own.

"Thank you for your kindness, Your Grace," she replied, a warm light in her eyes. "It has been a pleasure."

With that, the connection between them lingered in the air, an unspoken promise of understanding, a strengthening invisible thread that tugged at them. Isaac watched as Amelda turned to continue her task, transfixed for a while on the peculiar woman who had breezed into his life and captivated a portion of his mind.

He knew he should retreat back to the manor, to the responsibilities that awaited him, but a part of him longed to linger a little longer in her presence. As she walked away, he offered a final thought, "I hope to see you again, Amelda. Perhaps we could… explore the gardens together one day."

She paused, her back turned to him, and he could almost feel the warmth of her smile even from behind. "I would like that, Your Grace," she said, her words felt like a promise that they'd be able to talk again, and soon.

With that, she disappeared into the sprawling kitchens, leaving Isaac standing alone amidst the flowers and foliage.

The air felt different now, he felt different, as if he could summon from a well of courage not available before. The weight of his title still hung upon him, but the encounter had sparked something within him, he realised how much he desired to seek connection, to find meaning in the solitude he had come to accept here at Langston.

As he began to make his way back towards the manor, his thoughts spiralled. What would it mean to explore the depths of his own identity, to seek have a friend in this dratted loneliness? And while he felt so much surer and confident in the moment, he also felt on the precipice of a cliff, surrounded by the buffeting winds of the sea – a perilous drop below.

He knew he would seek Amelda out again, not only for the way she'd taken a corner of his mind, or that odd pull he felt towards her, for the easy joy of her company and to hear her thoughts. In that fleeting moment, he had glimpsed a world beyond the shadows and mists of the Blackwood curse, a world where stories could intertwine with reality – he believed she'd enjoy that too.

Chapter Six

The afternoon sun hung low over Langston Estate, casting a golden glow that illuminated the grand kitchen, bustling with activity. Amelda stood at the counter, kneading dough with hands, flour up to her elbows, her thoughts half-occupied with the meeting about to take place in the drawing room. The Duke had summoned the labourers to discuss their compensation and it had caused a stir to say the least.

As she rolled out the dough, she overheard the chatter of her fellow servants as they too were busy preparing food. The kitchen buzzed with anticipation, but it was not merely the talk of the meeting that caught Amelda's attention; it was the gossip about the Duke himself.

"Can you imagine what it'll be like when the Duke finally marries?" one of her fellow maids, Clara said, her voice lilting with excitement. "I wonder what kind of Lady of the Manor she'll be?"

"Probably someone haughty and cruel – most nobles tend to be," another maid chimed in, her tone dripping with disdain. She was older than the both of them and had served another family before coming to Langston. "Besides, who would want to marry a Blackwood, especially with that curse hanging over their heads?"

Amelda paused her work, momentarily intrigued. She had overheard similar conversations about the curse before but had never paid much attention. It felt like a euphemism for the peculiarities of the former, late Duke. Still, not many present had served in the household while there had been a Lady Blackwood. Mrs Henderson and Mrs Fletcher had, as had Williams, though he was busy elsewhere. She'd heard from all three how much they revered her memory, Mrs Henderson particularly.

"Or perhaps she'll be kind and gracious," Clara countered pointedly. "Imagine how different things could be if she truly cared for the people here like the last lady of the house. Mrs Henderson says Lady Florrie was too good for the likes of most noble society you know."

"But whoever she is," the third maid chimed in, "she'll have to be either foolhardy or completely unbothered by all this talk of curses. You do know your history right? It's not as if the curse only touches a Blackwood, it'll get her too."

Amelda felt her heart sink at the mention of this. She had read enough about it in the library to understand its apparent origins, and misfortune, madness, and tragedy that had befallen the family for generations. It was a subject shrouded in mystery enough that it was deemed important enough to note in that book she'd secreted back to the library after she'd finished it, but also one that her fellow servants discussed as though it were as true as the noses on their faces. The thought of marrying into such a legacy in that case, seemed daunting, even absurd.

"I know that the last duchess died far too young, and the one before her, not Duke Blackwood's grandmother – she was born a Blackwood, her mother in fact – she was quite mad before she passed," Clara continued. "You must admit, it doesn't sound appealing. I would hate to find myself in her position. It is odd that the curse kind of skipped a generation, maybe Duke Blackwood will be lucky, and his wife."

"More likely, she'll be years away," Mrs Henderson, the cook interjected, her voice gruff yet wise. "Who in their right mind would want to put up with you lot gossiping every second they get to spare? They'll need to find someone brave enough to ignore the whispers like our Lady Florrie was."

Amelda returned to her work, shaking her head slightly as she pushed the dough flat with the rolling pin. Although she had initially dismissed the curse as mere superstition, it was becoming increasingly difficult to ignore its implications.

The more she heard, the more she pondered how such tales might have shaped Isaac's life. At least she didn't have people gossiping about her and her future.

From her reading, she knew the Blackwood family had been plagued by ill luck. And those stories of woe had created an aura of fear, casting a long shadow over the estate just as real as any curse could be.

Yet, as she cut the pastry dough into small rounds, she couldn't help but wonder what sort of woman might eventually become the Duke's wife. Would she be brave enough to face the scrutiny of the staff, let alone the nonsense about the so called curse? She shook her head to dispel the thoughts, she was getting suckered into the gossip. Besides, it was all just stories to explain extraordinarily bad luck, wasn't it? The way they talked about it felt like it was more than mere stories though.

The talk of curses was loudly interrupted by the booming voice of Mr. Gatrell, one of the senior servants.

"Get on with your work, you lot!" he barked, crossing his arms over his chest. "The Duke's meeting won't wait for you to fill your heads nonsense about curses. And I'd rather not hear another word about any Lady Blackwood until she actually exists, we have a Duke to serve, not some imaginary wife. We have duties to fulfil in the here and now!"

The other servants hastily returned to their tasks, the air of small talk dissipating under Mr. Gatrell's authority. Amelda took a deep breath, shaking off her musings. She knew she had to keep focused. The refreshments needed to be perfect.

Once the pastries had turned a beautiful golden yellow and cooled, Amelda piped on the soft fluffy cream onto their tops, then arranged them neatly on a tray. Just as she was about to leave the kitchen, she heard the murmur of voices in the foyer outside the drawing room.

It was the labourers, a little earlier than expected for the evening meeting. She could see from their faces that there was a mixture of excitement and nervous energy in the group. She quickly espied a familiar face amongst them, and drew up beside him. His name was Rowland, a year or two her senior and he and his siblings had been friends with she and hers. They'd been almost neighbours, as he'd lived a few houses apart from them. They, she, her sister, Rowland, his sister, and several other children would all play together while their parents worked.

"Melly! Wait, no, you prefer Amelda don't you?" he smiled, his face brightening when he noticed her standing beside him. "It's been ages! How are you?"

She smiled, her heart warming at the sight of him. "You're taller than you last were Rowland, but I knew it was you! I'm well enough. Just busy, as always. How are you? Last I heard you'd taken to working in the fields?"

"Aye, well, I'm rather high up for just working in the fields these days, someone has to keep things running smoothly," he replied, a grin spreading across his face. "But it's good to see a familiar face here. Your ma said you'd gone to work as a servant, didn't know it was so close to home. Anyway, I heard about the Duke's meeting today figured I'd show up to see if it's all true, put my name down on the list when we made the petition for better pay after all so should see these things through. Must be quite something for him to sit down with us common folk though, eh?"

Amelda chuckled, her spirits lifting. He'd always spoken at a mile a minute, it was good that some things never changed. "Yes, I suppose it is. He seems determined to make changes for the better."

They shared a brief moment of basking in nostalgia, reminiscing about their childhood days spent chasing each other through the fields. But as the conversation flowed, Amelda couldn't shake the thought of the Duke from her mind. How different it must have been for him in these halls, how few peers he'd have had, and the cloying mist that soaked you through in autumn and chilled you to the bone in winter.

Several other servants had come to stand in the line besides the labourers as they chatted away, and she was silently thrilled at how good some of the refreshments looked. If there were any of the little cakes left when the meeting was done she'd ask if she could pinch one.

Just then, the door to the drawing room creaked open, and Isaac stepped into the hallway, his presence commanding attention. Amelda caught sight of him, her heart fluttering as he surveyed the room with an air of quiet control.

She could sense the shift in the atmosphere. The laughter and chatter faded to a respectful hush, replaced by the soft shuffle of feet. He greeted everyone as they entered the drawing room by name, which was met with pleasant shock by the older labourers.

They continued down the line together, Amelda with her tray and Rowland had removed his hat nervously. "It's Rowland Thomas yes? Good to meet you," Isaac said, he extended his hand and shook Rowland's with a friendliness that seemed to momentarily dispel the tension.

"Your Grace," Rowland replied, straightening up. He glanced briefly to Amelda beside him. "We were just speaking of the meeting while she brought in the pastries here. Nice to see an old friend get treated so well working for you."

Isaac nodded, his gaze drifting from Rowland until it settled on Amelda. For a brief moment, their eyes met, and she felt that strange connection between them that went past any words she could summon. He looked away, though, his brow furrowing slightly.

"Make sure everything is in order, will you?" Isaac said to her, turning back to Rowland. "I want to ensure the men are well taken care of during our discussions."

"Aye, Your Grace. I'm sure our Melly'll see to it," Rowland assured him, looking back at Amelda with a knowing smile before slipping back into the drawing room. She didn't let anyone but her family call her the childish nickname any more, but he had to push his luck.

As the door closed behind them, Amelda and the other servants busied themselves with setting the food and drinks about the table and the labourers seating themselves. It felt warm, cosy even. Yet that warmth quickly gave way to an unsettling thought: it had almost felt like jealousy – if she could be inclined to believe the Duke would be jealous that she had friends beyond him. She wasn't even sure if they were indeed friends yet, as they were so distant in stations that it could have just been a chivalrous nature in him and a yearning for human interaction that had let them talk so freely in the gardens the other day. It was ridiculous, she thought, and she tried to banish that errant notion.

She had a job to do, and for the moment, silly thoughts as well as all that chatter of the curse back in the kitchens would have to wait.

Isaac assumed his position at the head of the table. She moved quietly to the back of the room beside Clara and the maid that previously worked at another estate, but her mind was elsewhere, mulling over the conversations she had overheard in the kitchen. Not of the curse, the more real thing at least.

What kind of woman would eventually step into the role of Lady Blackwood? Amelda shared the hopes of Clara in that whoever she was, she'd be kind in the very least. And also not the sort to listen to rumours.

As Isaac spoke, his voice steady and authoritative, Amelda attempted to listen while she went about her duties with the other servants, catching snippets of the conversation. The way he engaged with the men, the respect he offered them – it was all very new, yet remarkably refreshing.

Yet, amidst it all, her thoughts drifted back to the curse that shadowed him. The tales she had heard echoed in her mind like the rustling of leaves in a restless wind. What would happen if the Duke actually was cursed, and his future wife too? That poor woman, if she died young or went mad that would be horrible! She knew from her sister that when a woman married she was hoping for love, for a lifetime with someone she trusted would care for her. Mary and Nelson had courted for so long while he'd travelled during his apprenticeship that the wedding almost felt like a formality compared to the bond they had nurtured. She often dreamed of having that same joy, as romantic as that would be.

As the discussions grew animated, Amelda felt an odd mix of admiration and concern for Isaac. It was clear he was doing his best to navigate a world that weighed heavily upon him. She could see behind the idealistic passion in his voice as he spoke that there was such a deep sadness etched into his face, all but screaming from his grey eyes.

And in that moment, she resolved once more to be the friend he needed – perhaps that was whatever jealousy she thought she'd felt – jealousy that someone else might so easily have friends. She'd be his friend as much as she was able, given their stations, because perhaps he desperately wanted nothing more than a break from all of this heartache, curse or not, that plagued him.

Chapter Seven

As the weeks unfolded at Langston Estate, the rhythm of life began to change for both Isaac and Amelda. Mrs Fletcher seemingly had little for the maid to do, so she'd been relegated back to the gardens and kitchens. The Duke had taken to exploring the estate on foot more often, seeking solace in the vast grounds that surrounded his ancestral home. Each day, he wandered deeper into the heart of the estate, where the lush greenery whispered secrets and the flowers bloomed in defiance of the heavy mists that lay upon them.

It was during one of these walks that Isaac crossed paths with Amelda again. He had been meandering along a winding path that led to the herb garden when he spotted her crouched down, her hands deftly pulling weeds from the soil. The sun shone upon her, casting a warm glow that accentuated the gentle curve of her profile as she worked, her brow slightly furrowed in concentration.

"Good afternoon, Amelda," he called, unable to suppress the smile that crept onto his lips.

She looked up, surprise lighting her features. "Your Grace! I didn't expect to see you here," she replied, her cheeks tinged with a delicate flush.

Isaac stepped closer, drawn as a moth to a flame to speak with the woman again, he noted that even with mud caking her fingers she managed to look the picture of the peace he sought. "I often find myself wandering the grounds," he admitted, glancing around at the chorus of colours that enveloped them. Despite the Langston mists the flowers bloomed, and he hoped that even he might become like them. "It's a welcome respite from the duties of the manor."

"It is a lovely place to escape to," Amelda agreed, standing up and brushing her hands against her apron. "The gardens have a way of putting things into perspective, don't they?"

"Indeed," he replied, his eyes sparkling with genuine interest. "What do you find most captivating about them?"

Amelda paused, her gaze drifting to the rows of flowers flourishing in the weak sun. "I think it's the way they grow despite the hardships they face – the weeds, the droughts, the mist. They remind me that there's beauty in resilience."

Isaac regarded her thoughtfully, impressed by the depth of her insight and how mirrored their thoughts were. "You have a way of seeing the world that is quite refreshing. I often feel as if I'm merely following the path laid out before me, but you –" he hesitated, searching for the right words. "I feel you must forge your own."

Amelda's heart quickened at his compliment, though she remained modest. "I suppose we all must try to find our own paths, no matter our circumstance," she replied, her tone steady.

"I envy that," he admitted, leaning against a nearby fence post. "There is so much expected of me as Duke. It feels at times as though I am encased in a gilded cage."

"I can only imagine," she said softly, a frown crossing her lips. "But there must be moments of joy amidst the weight."

"Perhaps," he mused, looking out at the distant trees swaying in the gentle breeze. "Moments like this, speaking with you, remind me of the joys that can exist alongside duty. I find myself longing for more conversations like this."

Amelda felt a flutter in her chest at his words, surprised by the honesty with which he spoke. "I would be glad to oblige," she said, unable to hide her smile. "I enjoyed our last talk, Your Grace."

"Isaac, please," he interjected, his expression earnest. "In these moments, there is no need for titles."

"Very well, Isaac," she replied, his name on her tongue sending a taboo thrill through her.

They continued to speak of literature, their shared interests emerging like tendrils of ivy intertwining. Amelda spoke of her favourite novels, her enthusiasm spilling over as she recounted the adventures of daring heroines. Isaac listened intently, offering the perspectives of those stories he knew of from the lecturers at the university.

"Do you believe that literature has the power to change one's perspective?" he asked, his eyes searching hers.

"Absolutely," she replied fervently. "Books allow us to experience lives and emotions we may never encounter otherwise. They can ignite our imaginations, incite great thoughts, and even inspire change."

Isaac nodded, his brow furrowed in contemplation. "Perhaps I ought to delve deeper into the world of literature. I believe you've inspired me to at the very least explore the library. It seems I have spent too long absorbed in the affairs of the estate without pausing to explore the world beyond."

"There is much to discover," Amelda encouraged. "You may find it a welcome reprieve from your responsibilities."

As their conversation continued, it was clear that they were both navigating uncharted waters, their connection deepening beneath the surface. Yet they were acutely aware of the boundaries set by their respective stations. There was a carefulness in their words, a respect for the propriety that dictated their interactions.

Over the following days, their paths crossed with increasing frequency. Amelda would often find herself in the gardens when Isaac wandered through, and they would engage in discussions that spanned the realms of duty, freedom, and the narratives that shaped their lives. Isaac was captivated by Amelda's intelligence and the warmth that radiated from her, and he began to anticipate their encounters with a longing that both excited and terrified him.

One afternoon, as the sun dipped low in the sky, painting the horizon in hues of orange and pink, Isaac found himself wandering along a path lined with towering oaks. He spotted Amelda seated on a bench, a book open on her lap, her brow furrowed in concentration.

"Amelda!" he called, his heart racing slightly as he approached.

She looked up, her face lighting up with delight. "Isaac! I was just getting lost in a story, it seemed nobody had a task for me so I thought I'd savour the moment. What brings you here?"

"I couldn't resist the call of the outdoors," he replied, sitting beside her. "And the lure of a good book, I see. What are you reading?"

She held the book up for him to see. "It's a novel about a woman who defies societal expectations to pursue her dreams as a knight of the realm. It's quite inspiring."

Isaac raised an eyebrow, intrigued. "And do you believe such defiance is possible? Can one truly forge their own path despite the constraints of society?"

Amelda thought for a moment, her gaze drifting to the words on the page before returning to his. "I believe it is possible, but it often comes at a cost. Freedom requires courage, and not everyone is willing to pay that price."

He regarded her with admiration, appreciating the depth of her reflections. "Courage seems to be a recurring theme in our conversations," he noted. "I wonder if I possess it myself."

"You do, whether you see it or not," she assured him, her voice firm yet gentle. "Taking steps towards change, especially in a position such as yours, requires immense bravery."

"Then I must endeavour to embody it more fully," he said, the weight of her words settling over him. "There are changes I wish to make, but the fear of repercussions often holds me back. I want a fairer world, and I feel like a sword where a pen should be."

Amelda leaned forward, her eyes bright with conviction. "You have the power to influence the lives of so many, Isaac. The courage to act is not merely personal; it can inspire others to find their own strength too – for all you know any reformations made in Langston could strike across the country like wildfire."

Isaac felt a surge of determination, her words igniting a flame within him. "Perhaps you are right. I've always been of the legacy which comes with the Blackwood name, but maybe I can be the light that dispels them."

Amelda smiled, her heart swelling with pride for him. "You can be, if you choose to embrace that courage you unknowingly have."

They sat in comfortable silence for a moment, the world around them fading as they shared their thoughts. Isaac couldn't help but notice the way the setting sun caught the strands of her hair, turning them to fire, and he felt a swell of something deeper, a yearning that was both exhilarating and frightening.

As the shadows lengthened and dusk began to settle, Amelda reluctantly closed her book. "I should return to the kitchen, I've likely overstated my availability to read," she said, the reluctance in her voice evident.

"Will you be in the gardens again tomorrow?" he asked, his heart racing at the thought of another encounter.

"Of course," she replied, her smile brightening the dimming light. "I look forward to it."

As Amelda walked away, Isaac felt a mix of elation and apprehension. He was drawn to her radiance and intelligence, yet he knew the boundaries that separated them – the divide of rank and duty. And yet, he couldn't shake the feeling that what they shared was more than mere friendship.

Over the next few days, their conversations grew even more profound. They began to explore the themes of duty and freedom, discussing the complexities of the choices they faced. Isaac spoke of the expectations placed upon him as Duke, the pressures to conform to the traditions that had governed the Blackwood family for generations.

"There are days I feel like a puppet," he confessed one afternoon as they strolled through the meadows. "My actions are dictated by a lineage I did not choose. How does one break free from that?"

Amelda pondered his words, her heart aching for him. "You can start by defining what you want for yourself, separate from your title. It's not easy, but it is necessary. Your life is yours to shape, not just the legacy you inherit."

Isaac looked at her, appreciation flooding his senses. "You make it sound so simple. But I fear the repercussions of such decisions. What if I fail?"

"Failure is simply a part of life," Amelda said gently. "It's how we learn and grow. Don't let the fear of failure dictate your choices. Instead, let your heart guide you."

As they spoke, the connection between them deepened. Isaac found himself captivated not only by her words but by the way she viewed the world, fearlessly and with hope. It was a stark contrast to the weight he carried, and it stirred something within him, a desire to embrace that same hope.

One evening, as twilight descended and painted the sky in shades of purple, Amelda was leaving the kitchen gardens, her hands still warm from the day's work. She brushed her apron clean, preparing to head back to her small room when she spotted Isaac leaning against a tree, a bottle of red wine cradled in one hand and a delicate glass in the other. The scene struck her as unexpected; it was a rare sight to see the Duke so casually engaged in something so informal.

"Good evening, Your Grace," she greeted, her tone light yet respectful. "I hope I'm not interrupting."

Isaac looked up, a grin spreading across his face. "Not at all, Amelda. In fact, I could use some company. Care for a drink?"

Amelda hesitated, the notion of sharing a drink with the Duke stirring a mixture of intrigue and caution within her. "I can't, I'm afraid," she replied, shaking her head. "It wouldn't be appropriate."

"Just a sip?" he pressed, tilting the bottle toward her in invitation. "I assure you, it's not a grand affair. Just two people enjoying a moment away from the expectations of our lives."

The weight of propriety bore down on her, yet she felt a pull toward his earnestness. She took a seat on the grass beside him, grateful for the chance to escape the confines of her duties. "You certainly make it tempting, Isaac," she said, allowing herself a small smile. "But truly, I must decline."

"Very well, then," he said, pouring himself a glass and taking a sip, his gaze fixed on the horizon where the sun had dipped below the trees. "But I do enjoy our conversations. There's a sense of freedom here, don't you think?"

Amelda nodded, the easy bond they shared coiling around them. "Yes, it's nice to share a moment away from the walls of the manor."

As they sat in companionable silence, the soft sounds of nature enveloping them, Isaac turned to her. "Tell me, Amelda, how did you come to be so much wiser than I am? I often find myself at a loss when it comes to matters of the heart and mind."

She laughed, the sound light and musical in the stillness of the evening. "Wiser? I certainly don't feel wise," she replied, a glimmer of self-deprecation in her eyes. "I'm just a girl trying to make sense of the world."

"But you see it so clearly," he insisted, his expression earnest. "What's your secret?"

Amelda leaned back on her hands, considering his question. "I suppose it's all about perspective. We each carry memories that shape our views. Mine, for instance, is of my mother."

"Your mother?" Isaac echoed, intrigued. "What's the memory?"

A smile tugged at Amelda's lips as she remembered. "I recall the evenings when she would mend shirts by candlelight. My elder sister would read stories to keep us entertained while my mother worked. The light would flicker, casting shadows on the walls, and I felt safe. It taught me the value of hard work and the joy that can be found in any moment."

Isaac's gaze softened, the sincerity of her memory resonating with him. "That sounds lovely. I feel my views are quite stark from yours. If I can share, my own memory is rather bittersweet. It was the last time I saw my father before leaving for the capital. He held me tight, as if he knew it was the last we'd see of each other. He was so proud, but I could see the worry in his eyes. He wasn't an affectionate man by nature so even that embrace – it felt to foreign to me that it stands out."

"He appeared worried?" Amelda prompted gently.

"Yes," he admitted. "I'm sure he feared for my future, for what awaited me in the world of politics and duty. He let me go, and I knew that the weight of my family's legacy rested on my shoulders."

"That must be a heavy burden," she said softly. He looked down at her from where he stood and sat himself a short distance away, half in the shadow of the tree.

"It was," he replied, the headiness of the wine freeing a kind of vulnerability from him. "I find myself thinking of that courage you said you see in me, and how perhaps courage is not merely in bearing such burdens, but in daring to change one's lot in life."

Amelda considered this, her heart stirring with the thought. "And what will you choose to do with that courage?"

Isaac met her gaze, it was an ancient spark he felt, revolutionary. "I want to make a difference, Amelda. Not just for my family's name, but for the people of this estate. And perhaps, one day, for those beyond its borders."

"You have the heart for it," she encouraged, happiness bubbling in her chest. "But remember, true bravery is often found in vulnerability. In opening oneself to the possibilities of failure and growth."

Isaac nodded, feeling the weight of her words settle in his mind. "And what about you? How will you choose to wield your wisdom that you cannot see in yourself?"

Amelda smiled. "I'll continue to learn from the past, cherish the present, and dare to dream of a future filled with possibilities, even if it seems far-fetched."

As the stars twinkled above them, they sat in silence, each pondering the paths that lay ahead. In that fleeting moment, surrounded by the beauty of nature, the gyre that was between them and their stations seemed so arbitrary as to be non-existent, they were simply two people sharing a moment together.

Chapter Eight

The morning sun filtered through the trees, mottling the ground with patches of warm light as Isaac made his way along an overgrown path of Langston Estate. Williams had made sure that his morning walks at the very least were accompanied in some way, or guarded would have been a more correct term. The gamekeeper would somehow always be nearby enough that he wasn't alone per se, though he certainly felt alone as the man never spoke to him or acknowledged the extra duty the head butler had given him. The air was crisp, filled with the earthy scents of dew-kissed grass and blooming wildflowers. He relished these almost-solitary walks, where he could escape the weight of his title and the expectations that accompanied it. Today, however, there was an unsettling quiet in the air, a tension that made him acutely aware of his surroundings.

Isaac strolled deeper into the woods that bordered the estate, a place he often sought solace. The tall oaks and ancient pines stood like sentinels, their branches swaying gently in the breeze. He paused for a moment, taking a deep breath, letting the cool air fill his lungs. It was a small moment of peace, one that he cherished in the midst of a life governed by duty and decorum.

As he continued on, Isaac allowed his thoughts to drift to Amelda. Their conversations had become a lifeline, a connection he never knew he craved. The way she spoke, with such insight and care would leave him feeling both inspired and intrigued. Each exchange peeled back the layers of his carefully constructed façade, revealing a longing that was unexpected. But the weight of his title kept him from voicing those thoughts, leaving him to ponder and yearn in silence at what the nature of their connection could be.

Suddenly, a loud crack echoed through the stillness of the woods, startling him from his reverie. Isaac glanced up, just in time to see a large branch breaking free from a nearby oak tree. The world around him slowed, the branch falling in an arc that felt like an eternity. In a split second, instinct kicked in, and he dove to the side, narrowly avoiding the deadly trajectory of the wood where it staked the mud where he'd stood.

He landed hard on the ground, the wind knocked from his lungs. The sound reverberated through the trees, and for a moment, all was silent except for the rapid thud of his heartbeat. Isaac lay there, his heart racing, the weight of the near-miss crashing over him like a tidal wave.

Pushing himself up, he looked at the massive branch that now lay splintered beside him, its bark rough and unforgiving. Shaking, he gathered himself, the reality of the close call sinking in. What had just happened? Had it really been an accident?

A chill ran down his spine as the thought of the curse crossed his mind. Perhaps it wasn't just a collection of unfortunate coincidences after all. He noticed, ever so briefly, the gamekeeper a short distance away, though certainly couldn't make out his expression, and the man did not approach.

Isaac took a moment to steady himself, rubbing his hands against his trousers to dispel the lingering shock. He pushed to his feet and retraced his steps, moving more cautiously this time. The woods felt different now, the shadows longer, the air heavier. It was as if the trees themselves were aware of the legacy of darkness that clung to his family name.

When he returned to the estate, he found the usual bustle of servants preparing for the day's tasks. But today, a noticeable shift hung in the air, whispers and furtive glances exchanged like a secret code. Isaac caught snippets of conversation as he passed through the corridors, the words "accident" and "curse" echoing off the stone walls. So it wasn't being guarded, it was merely being watched. And the gamekeeper had already told someone with a loud mouth or enough people that the news had spread quickly.

He walked toward the kitchens, where the heart of the estate throbbed with activity. Amelda was there, her sleeves rolled up as she chopped vegetables, her focus unwavering. He hadn't even noticed how he'd instinctively gone straight to her, but his mind was elsewhere. It wasn't even on how improper it could be to simply stroll into the kitchen. Even she seemed aware of the atmosphere, her movements punctuated by the occasional glance toward the door, as if expecting someone – or something. He took a moment to observe her before he let himself be seen.

"Good morning, Your Grace," she said brightly, though her eyes betrayed a hint of concern as her eyes raked across his features. "You're back early from your walk."

"Yes," he replied, forcing a smile despite the lingering unease from the incident. "A bit of a close call, I suppose."

"A close call?" Amelda set down her knife, turning to face him fully. The worry etched on her features was palpable. "What do you mean?" So the news hadn't reached the kitchens yet? He'd outrun it somehow.

Isaac hesitated, unsure how much to reveal what had happened. "A branch fell. I managed to avoid it, but it was... startling, to say the least."

Amelda's expression shifted, concern deepening. "Are you hurt?" She stepped closer, inspecting him as if expecting to find physical evidence of his ordeal.

"I'm fine, truly. Just shaken," he assured her. But in that moment, he saw the flicker of fear in her eyes. It stirred something within him – a desire to protect her from the burden of the family curse, even as it weighed on him. He wasn't sure why he'd have to protect her, because insofar as he knew, it never actually touched any of the servants.

"Do you think it was just an accident?" she asked quietly, her voice almost a whisper. He knew what she meant of course.

"I don't know," Isaac admitted, the uncertainty heavy on his chest. It couldn't have been done on purpose – he'd have seen saw marks on the branch at the very least. "It could be. Or it could be... something more. The curse is talked about often enough. It makes one wonder."

Amelda frowned, a hint of frustration crossing her features. "You can't let the stories dictate your life, Isaac. They're just that – stories. Bad luck can happen to anyone, but that doesn't mean it's a sign of something sinister."

"Perhaps you're right," he said, appreciating her lack of belief, it was his prevailing theory that this was what had saved his grandparents such ill fortune. "But… it's hard to dismiss when it's so deeply ingrained in the history of my family."

The kitchen door swung open, and several other servants entered, their chatter halting abruptly as they caught sight of Isaac. The whispers began anew, this time more pronounced and tinged with apprehension. Isaac felt the weight of their gaze, an unspoken fear that resonated through the room.

"Did you hear?" one of the maids said to another, her voice barely above a whisper. "They say the curse is awakening. The Duke nearly lost his life today!"

Amelda stiffened at the words, her eyes darting to Isaac before she quickly resumed her task. Isaac felt the sting of her glance, a mixture of sympathy and concern, but also something deeper. Presumably the maid didn't realise how far her voice carried.

"Is everything prepared for the afternoon's tasks?" he asked, attempting to shift the focus away from himself and the lurking shadows of superstition. He also needed a good reason to be in the kitchens.

"Yes, Your Grace," another servant replied, bowing slightly, though her eyes were wide with curiosity. "Just about ready."

"Good," Isaac said, his voice steady. "Let's ensure the day proceeds without further interruptions."

As he stepped away from the kitchen, he could hear the whispers behind him, speculations about the curse that had haunted his family for generations no doubt. The shadow of its influence loomed larger with each passing moment.

Amelda's voice cut through the tension as she spoke to the other servants. "It's not wise to dwell on such things. You have an oven to get to temperature don't you? That bread shan't cook itself! Just because Mrs Henderson is on leave is not an excuse to slack."

Isaac turned back to see her standing firm, a glint of defiance in her eyes. He admired her for it; she seemed to embody a kind of courage that he struggled to summon. Perhaps that was what drew him to her – her unwavering strength that he craved in himself.

Later that afternoon, as the sun slipped lower in the sky, Isaac found himself in the drawing room, surrounded by the remnants of what looked to be a productive day. Yet, the usual sense of accomplishment eluded him. He couldn't shake the feeling of impending doom, as if the curse had awakened from its slumber to remind him of its presence.

He poured himself a glass of wine, the rich liquid swirling like his thoughts. Was it true? Did the curse truly have a grip on him? His ancestors had suffered immensely, and now, with the weight of his title heavy on his shoulders, he felt more trapped than ever.

Amelda's laughter echoed in his mind, a sweet sound that momentarily dispelled the dark clouds gathering overhead. She had a way of making the weight of the world feel a little lighter, of coaxing light from the shadows.

Later that evening, when Amelda returned from her duties, he found himself unwittingly seeking her out again. "Amelda," he called, spotting her in the hall as she carried a basket filled with freshly laundered linens. "Can we talk for a moment?"

"Of course, Your Grace," she replied, placing the basket down and wiping her hands on her apron.

"I wanted to thank you for your words earlier," he said, his voice earnest. "It's easy to get lost in the whispers, but you remind me that I can choose how to respond to them."

She regarded him with a thoughtful expression. "I'm glad to hear that, Isaac. The curse may be a part of your family's history, real or not, but it doesn't have to define you."

Isaac felt a flicker of hope in her words, a reminder that he was not alone in this struggle. "I wish I had your confidence," he admitted.

Amelda smiled softly. "Confidence comes with experience. You have to face your fears head-on, even if it's daunting. Just like that branch earlier – an accident can happen to anyone, but it's how we respond that truly matters."

Their conversation flowed, a soothing balm against the uncertainty that had begun to settle in his heart. As the evening wore on, he found himself sharing more of his thoughts and fears, the barriers between them dissolving like mist in the morning sun.

Yet, in the back of his mind, the whispers of the curse remained, an ever-present reminder of the darkness that lingered.

Isaac strolled through the eastern edge of the Langston forest, with the sharp scent of pine needles filling the air and the earthy crunch of leaves beneath his boots. At his side walked Mr Cropp, the gamekeeper, a sturdy man in his fifties with a weathered face and a keen eye for the land. Over the past few days, Cropp and Mr Gatrell, one of the senior servants, had been carefully inspecting the forest, checking each tree for any signs of weakness or decay.

Isaac, ever since the close call with the fallen branch, felt an odd unease whenever he ventured among the trees he once found solace in, and it was clear to him that some precautions needed to be taken.

As they reached a small clearing, Cropp stopped and tipped his cap to Isaac, brushing a rough hand across his grizzled beard. "Your Grace, we've gone through most of the grove along the east path and further down by the brook," he began, pointing to the trees they had marked. "Any limb that looked precarious, me and Gatrell went at it with saw and shears. And any tree showing signs of rot, well, we've put them on a list to be felled come spring."

Isaac nodded, the familiar tension in his shoulders easing. "Thank you, Cropp. I appreciate the thoroughness; it's reassuring to know the land's been seen to with such care. I wouldn't want another incident." His voice was even, but his mind flickered briefly to the strange dread that had settled in him since that day. The estate, though his inheritance, had seemed almost antagonistic of late, as though reminding him that he was treading upon land soaked with his family's blood.

"Aye, Your Grace," Cropp replied, his gaze steady. "Langston's woods are wild, but she'll mind herself if we mind her first." He looked around, taking in the dappled sunlight filtering through the branches above. "There's a life to it, the forest, same as any creature. If you respect it, it'll respect you back. That's what my father used to say, and his father before him." He paused, then added with a touch of warmth, "So you needn't worry yourself, sir. You've got Gatrell and me on your side, and we'll see to it that you're safe out here."

A smile touched Isaac's lips as he glanced around the forest, now dappled filled with the soft summer light. "I'm in good hands, then. I'd be lost without the wisdom of men who know these lands better than I do," he said. "I'll take care to respect the forest's... character." The two shared a brief nod of understanding, Isaac realising how deeply the estate's staff understood Langston's needs, perhaps even more so than he did.

Chapter Nine

Isaac found himself drawn to the muted light of his study, a space where his father had spent countless hours in near silence, poring over documents by flickering candlelight as the rain lashed against the windows. Now, in the middle of the day, a subdued grey light seeped through the long, heavily draped windows, settling onto the neatly stacked letters and notices that littered the desk. The study was far less grand than other rooms of Langston Manor; it was modest, severe in its arrangements, much like his father had been. Now, even days after the accident, Isaac felt a coldness in his spine when he recalled that moment in the woods, the sharp crack of the branch above him, the sight of splintered wood only inches from where he'd stumbled back in the nick of time. Even the assurances of Mr Cropp, the gamekeeper, could not truly quell his fears.

"Is this the curse?" he found himself muttering as he leaned against the broad, leather-backed chair behind the desk, which still smelled faintly of the pipe smoke his father had once favoured. The accident had left him shaken in a way he hadn't expected, stirring within him an anxious thoughtfulness that gnawed at him, especially now with so much left to settle.

The household was a hive of movement, preparing Langston for what would be the final part of his father's traditional mourning rites. In Briarvale's tradition, families of high standing often held the last gathering of the mourning season with a certain solemnity, inviting those who had known the deceased or who held familial ties. The day marked the official end of the dark veils and half-mast standards, ushering in a symbolic return to life. His father's distant relations were arriving by the day, bringing with them what felt like both old ghosts and fresh judgements. Most of the guests would stay only until the ball, a gathering where he would greet Briarvale's nobility on behalf of his family, presenting himself as the new Duke of Blackwood.

Two particular arrivals weighed heavily on Isaac's mind: his mother's distant cousin, Basil Brisley, and his father's cousin, Theodore Blackwood. They were men of very different statures and reputations, but both seemed keenly aware that should Isaac fail to produce an heir, the Blackwood title might pass into their hands. Basil Brisley, a lord of modest holdings to the west, held himself with a particular disdain that Isaac had noticed even as a boy; Basil had always spoken of Langston's grandeur with a longing that thinly veiled his envy. His letters had come promptly with the news of Augustus's passing, full of elaborate language about "family duty" and a willingness to "support" Isaac should it be required.

Then there was Theodore Blackwood, a quiet, observant man who served as a magistrate in the capital. His air of austere professionalism was tempered by a slight awkwardness around Isaac, as if the authority he so confidently wielded in court had little bearing within the walls of Langston. Theodore was a man driven by duty, but he had rarely ventured outside of his role, rarely visited family, and certainly had never shown much sentiment towards the estate or the title.

Isaac had spoken little to either man since his formative years, and with the fresh whispers among the servants about his "accident," the weight of their impending presence settled uneasily over him. They would both be at the gathering, observing him, perhaps even scrutinising him, but for now, he was grateful for the solitude that lingered, fleeting though it was, in the study.

A sharp knock on the door startled him out of his reverie, and he called for them to enter, bracing himself in case it was yet another visitor.

"Apologies, Your Grace," Williams entered with a slight bow. He noted that the man's grey hair was ever so slightly out of it's usual neatly combed look, his voice was ever so hoarse as well, and his cheeks pinker. "Lord Brisley and Magistrate Blackwood have arrived. They're being shown to their rooms and requested an audience when it suits you."

Isaac nodded, the tension in his shoulders hardening. "Thank you, Williams. I suppose I ought to greet them now, if they're not too weary from travel."

Williams hesitated, clearly discerning Isaac's reluctance. "Very good, sir. Shall I have refreshments prepared in the parlour?"

"Yes, thank you," Isaac replied, forcing a polite smile. He knew the arrival of his kin meant the start of more than one exhausting conversation. "And, Williams," he added as the butler turned to leave, "what have you heard among the staff about... the incident?"

Williams straightened, his expression briefly giving way to a more personal concern. "The servants have spoken of it, sir, as I'm sure you expected. It's been... speculated upon, shall we say, and no small number seem to believe it's a sign of the curse taking hold."

Isaac forced a laugh, though it felt hollow, mirthless. "Of course. Nothing else could possibly explain it, could it?"

Williams offered a sympathetic nod. "Indeed, sir. They will be watching closely, I think. But they are also quite loyal, as you know."

"Yes, I know," Isaac replied, with a deep breath, wondering if loyalty could counter the fear that seemed to hang like a mist over the estate.

The night of the mourning ball arrived, bringing a tide of familiar and unfamiliar faces to Langston. The large hall, draped in sombre colours and adorned with the Blackwood crest in solemn black-and-silver bunting, hummed with the murmurs of nobles who, despite the supposed solemnity, seemed eager for a glimpse of both Isaac and the curse rumoured to haunt his family. Here and there, Isaac noticed guests leaning in close, sharing whispers that travelled in guarded tones across the hall like a growing breeze.

Isaac, positioned near the central staircase with a clear view of the room, held a glass in his hand, though he had barely touched it. He was acutely aware of every look cast his way, of every hushed laugh and murmured comment. Though they kept up appearances with pleasant words when he greeted them, the undercurrent of curiosity and intrigue was unmistakable.

"Another accident, I heard!" one woman said, too loudly, and her voice carried even as her companion shushed her, her eyes darting toward Isaac.

"Can you imagine?" replied her friend, her voice thick with feigned pity. "They say the branch was an inch from his head. I'd say he's lucky to be here tonight at all."

Isaac turned away, suppressing the anger welling within him. Were they genuinely concerned, he wondered, or simply fascinated by the supposed curse, happy to have something to discuss beyond the mundanity of their own lives? He could not tell if their curiosity was born of true sympathy or if they were merely intrigued by the grotesque possibility of a noble family cursed by their own hubris.

Out of the corner of his eye, he spotted Lord Brisley, who was making his way through the crowd in Isaac's direction, gesturing emphatically to his companions as he passed. Brisley's gaze lit up when he caught sight of Isaac, and he made a show of excusing himself from his current conversation, heading over with what appeared to be barely-contained glee.

"Isaac!" he greeted, far louder than necessary. He clapped a firm hand on Isaac's shoulder. "Your Grace! A sombre night indeed – but how good it is to see you here, standing strong after that harrowing accident."

Isaac's jaw tightened, but he forced himself to smile and return the greeting with some semblance of warmth. "Thank you, Lord Brisley. I assure you, I am quite well."

"Yes, yes, of course. But you must admit, there are those who are more…well, let us say, prone to believe in certain tales," Brisley said, his voice dropping to a conspiratorial murmur. He leaned in, eyes glinting with amusement. "People have been talking, you know, and who am I to quell their fancies? A family curse! It's the most gripping tale one could imagine. Keeps everyone on their toes, doesn't it?"

Isaac's smile faltered, though Brisley didn't seem to notice, continuing on in his theatrical manner, gesturing wildly as he recounted tales of "cursed" estates he'd heard of during his travels. He seemed blissfully unaware, or perhaps indifferent, to Isaac's discomfort, clearly enjoying the attention he was receiving by association with the Blackwood rumours.

"Still," Brisley continued, "you know I've always said it— there's nothing quite as thrilling as a curse to bring a little life to a family name, wouldn't you say? Not that you believe in such nonsense, of course."

Isaac inclined his head. "One must be cautious with beliefs, Lord Brisley. The power of suggestion can be a dangerous thing."

Brisley laughed heartily, either not catching or wilfully ignoring the edge in Isaac's tone. "Well, of course! A sensible man like yourself would never fall prey to such fancies." He clapped Isaac on the back again, harder this time. "And, if I may say, it's good to see a Blackwood with such composure. I hope you know that I'm here to support you, should you ever need counsel."

Isaac thanked him, doing his best to make his gratitude seem genuine, and watched as Brisley turned back to the crowd, already launching into a new story about a supposed haunted estate he'd once visited.

Relieved to be momentarily free from Brisley's theatrics, Isaac turned and caught sight of another familiar face at the edge of the room. Theodore Blackwood stood there, watching him quietly, an untouched glass of wine in his hand. Where Brisley was all bluster and show, Theodore was calm and unreadable, his presence subtle, almost fading into the background. Isaac made his way over, welcoming the steadiness Theodore seemed to radiate.

"Theodore," Isaac greeted him, offering a handshake.

"Your Grace," Theodore replied, his expression softening slightly with a nod. He studied Isaac, his gaze steady, as though assessing him with a mix of caution and care. Though they shared a family name, he was a very distant relation, his great-uncle's grandson. Had his own grandmother not inherited the title of Duchess, it would be likely that their positions in life would be quite opposite each other.

"Thank you for coming," Isaac said. "I know these gatherings are not… enjoyable for everyone."

Theodore inclined his head. "They are a necessity," he replied. "Family duty, after all." He paused, his gaze sharpening. "I've heard about the accident."

Isaac exhaled, nodding. "Yes. I've heard about little else all evening."

Theodore's gaze lingered on Isaac's face, as if searching for any sign of alarm or fear. "Are you well?"

Isaac hesitated. "Physically, yes. But the estate feels… different, Theodore. The air, the atmosphere. It's difficult to describe."

Theodore nodded slowly, a faint flicker of understanding in his eyes. "The mind plays tricks in times of grief and transition. Langston has been through much – more than most homes. It would be foolish to dismiss your concerns entirely, but perhaps it is merely… the remnants of a dark season."

Isaac considered his cousin's words, finding an unexpected comfort in them. Theodore, unlike Brisley, neither dismissed nor amplified his fears. He met Isaac's gaze with a level of honesty that Isaac had rarely encountered among his family. Theodore summered at Langston when they'd been children, and he'd looked forward to having a playmate close to his age.

"You've chosen a difficult path," Theodore added quietly. "But you're handling it with grace, more than most would."

Isaac managed a small smile, grateful for Theodore's pragmatism. "Thank you, Theodore. That means a great deal."

The two men fell into a brief, companionable silence, watching the swirl of the crowd before Theodore took his leave to the suite the servants had put him in, he was as unobtrusive in leaving as he had arrived.

As the evening drew to a close, Isaac made his way up to his study, where the solitude beckoned to him like an old friend. He poured himself a measure of brandy and sat down in the same chair his father had favoured, the weight of the evening settling over him. More than ever he wished for the company of Amelda. He hadn't pried with Mrs Fletcher or Williams on where her duties had taken her for today, but he sorely missed the comfort of her smiles, her easy, quiet strength, her quick mind, and as his mind began to wander with the brandy filling it, he missed the way her hair shone red in the weak sunlight, and the way her eyes peered into his soul and met him more an equal than their stations would let them otherwise.

Chapter Ten

Amelda found much solace in the Langston Estate's library, the scent of aged paper was comforting, as were the books themselves. Most of the nobles who'd attended the ball the prior night were sleeping hangovers off, so duties were light in the kitchen that Mrs Fletcher had put her to work on cleaning. Williams had mentioned the library needed dusting, acting as her co-conspirator in the pursuit of reading, but she jumped at the chance to while away some hours in there before she was actually needed. The high, arched windows allowed beams of sunlight to filter through, illuminating the dust motes that danced lazily in the air. She was supposed to be tidying the shelves and organising the myriad tomes that had accumulated over the years. They were long overdue being sorted properly. Yet her heart wasn't truly in the task. Instead, she wandered through the labyrinth of books, her fingers brushing against the spines, yearning to escape into the worlds contained within.

While arranging a stack of oversized volumes on a low shelf where it could take their weight, Amelda noticed something peculiar peeking out from between the shelves – a small, leather-bound journal, faded and worn. Curiosity piqued, she carefully pulled it free and settled into a plush armchair nearby, eager to uncover its secrets.

She opened the journal to reveal pages yellowed with age, filled with elegant cursive writing. The ink had faded somewhat but still retained a certain allure, drawing her in as if beckoning her to uncover long-buried secrets.

The first few entries chronicled mundane details of life in the Blackwood household – family gatherings, the changing of the seasons, and the various entertainments of the nobility. But as she continued to read, the tone shifted dramatically. The writer, a Duke of Blackwood, began to pour out his heart, detailing an affair with a woman who was not ever to be accepted by the landed gentry.

Amelda's pulse quickened as she immersed herself in the words. The Duke had fallen deeply in love with a beautiful woman – the daughter of an alchemist he'd written, he wrote of how they shared the same soul, how they let the flames of their passion mingle. It was almost risqué. However, as she read on, societal expectations weighed heavily upon him, and he ultimately succumbed to the pressure of an arranged marriage to a lady of noble blood. The anguish of the Duke's choice leaped from the pages, each word steeped in regret.

As the story unfolded, Amelda felt a chill creep up her spine. The journal described a devastating confrontation with his former lover, who cursed him in a fit of despair, vowing that he would suffer for his betrayal. "May the Blackwood line forever know the pain etched in my heart" she had shouted, her words seemed to echo off the journal where the ancient Duke had recorded it. Amelda could all but feel the words leaping out of the page, and imagined a confrontation on a stormy cliff, rain battering down on a duo that had been separated. It was said that hate and love were different sides of the same coin and she could feel how true it was in her imagination of the event.

Amelda's brow furrowed as she continued to read. The journal recounted the curse that had befallen the Blackwood family since that fateful day. The original Duke noted each tragedy that befell him, how his wife and all but one of his children dying in mysterious circumstances, and how he felt stricken with visions of the dead each night, needing copious potions and elixirs to even drift off to sleep. He worried that with such strong proof of the curse he'd received being real – his surviving heir, a daughter, would also receive it. How each generation of Dukes and Duchesses who dared to reach for greatness would be doomed to eternal misery, plagued by misfortune and sorrow.

Amelda recalled the history book she'd read not long after Isaac had come to the estate and how it revealed a lineage marked by heartbreak, madness, and despair. Though with that, she recalled the skipped generation, Isaac's grandparents. They'd somehow been marked as different compared to their ancestors or their own sons. That book had said it was some dark ritual or pact made by the first Duke Blackwood of Langston, not a scorned lover with twisted magic cursing them.

As she turned the pages of the journal until she reached it's bitter end, Amelda pondered the implications of this curse on Isaac. At this point, she was feeling more sure that it existed, and she worried that the Duke, with his idealistic reformations in his head and heart might be invoking that curse. It was what the first Duke believed. Surely this curse was only affecting certain Blackwoods, and if the journal was correct – why had it not actually touched Isaac's grandparents, what marked them as different? She tried to think on what the actual history book seemed to chronicle, as it was collated with more information than the first Duke had to hand.

She recalled that most of the misfortunes started to occur after they'd wedded, or assumed the title. He was not courting anyone; his heart remained untouched as far as she knew. They were friends so she assumed he'd have told her if he was writing to someone to court. But the weight of legacy hung heavily on him, and she couldn't help but wonder if his accident was merely that or the curse. If it was, then surely it was happening far too soon – as if his fate were sealed already. That made her heart hurt, as he spoke so fervently of changing his path in life. But that sea of troubles could not be easy to bear, and she certainly understood why he'd accept his lot in life. Most had to eventually.

A sense of foreboding settled in Amelda's chest as she closed the journal and secreted it into her apron. She felt as if she had uncovered a secret that should remain hidden, a piece of history that was not hers to disclose. There was an alcove in the attic that would keep the journal safe for now – she didn't wish for Isaac to uncover it himself and have more troubles upon him. Yet, the weight of it lingered in her mind, casting a shadow over her thoughts. She'd have to bring it up carefully to him, one day when things were less chaotic or stressful.

Isaac was in his study, surrounded by the remnants of the recent ball which for him, was a mild hangover and a half-finished glass of wine which sat abandoned on the polished desk. The musky scent of funerary flowers that had been decorations still lingered in the air, which he was thankful for as without it he had no doubt there would be a sickly fug emanating from the guest rooms. His room was a sanctuary, filled with leather-bound volumes and papers scattered across the surface. He had hoped to enjoy a moment of peace, but his thoughts were clouded with the recent conversation he had overheard among the servants.

The door creaked open, and Lord Brisley sauntered in, a self-satisfied grin plastered across his face. He looked no worse for wear, though had definitely outpaced most of the drinkers last night. "Ah, Duke Blackwood! How fortuitous to find you here," he said, his tone oozing with insincerity. "I wanted to have a word about your future seeing as we didn't get much of a chance last night."

Isaac raised an eyebrow, instantly on guard. "My future? I don't recall asking for your counsel, Brisley."

"Of course not," Brisley replied, unabashed. "But as your, ahem, friend, I thought it wise to remind you that it is customary for a man of your standing to marry within a year of assuming his title. You must have been told of this tradition so to speak. Surely you wouldn't want to incur the wrath of the King, would you?"

Isaac's expression hardened at the reminder. He was aware of the tradition, if his governesses hadn't told him, he'd have learned about it in his education. He'd tried to keep it out of his mind for the most part. "I have no intentions of rushing into marriage, especially not to appease the King or anyone else."

Brisley leaned against the door frame, a smirk playing on his lips. "That's quite bold of you, Isaac. But consider the advantages of a strategic alliance. Marrying a lady of noble blood could bolster your position immensely. A strong marriage can serve as a powerful political tool."

"I understand the implications, Brisley," Isaac replied, his voice strained. "But I won't enter into a union simply for convenience or duty. I want –" he hesitated, searching for the right words. He didn't even know why he felt like saying it to the man. "I want something real. Something that isn't dictated by obligation or expectation."

Brisley crossed his arms, his amusement fading. "I appreciate your idealism, Isaac, but you must also recognise the reality of your situation. The nobility thrives on connections and alliances. Your marriage could strengthen ties with other powerful families, not to mention the political implications that come with it. Curse be damned, there will be ladies lining up to court."

Isaac leaned back in his chair, running a hand through his hair in frustration. "You make it sound so mercenary. What of love, Brisley? What of finding someone with whom I can share my life? Am I to simply sacrifice my happiness at the altar of duty?"

Brisley shrugged, his expression shifting to one of seriousness. "You may find that love often follows the path of duty, my friend. It certainly did for me. I couldn't stand my wife when we first met. Children make it easier. Besides, think of your father – he married into my family for political reasons, did he not, and he was a well respected Duke. Would you prefer to be remembered for your ideals or your lineage?"

Isaac's jaw clenched at the mention of his father. Respect – sure – his father had been respected by much of the nobility, though none truly knew the fear and madness that gripped him nor the uncloseable distance he'd kept from his own son. The weight of traditions he'd been born into hung over him and was a bitter reminder of the past. "My father's choices don't dictate my own. I refuse to be shackled by his legacy, nor the trappings that apparently define a noble. I will not be a puppet on strings."

Brisley pushed himself away from the door and straightened, his expression turning earnest. "Then you must take matters into your own hands, find your love if you so wish it, but do so with haste. And if you wish to avoid the King's displeasure, you need to make your intentions known to the eligible ladies of the gentry. It would be wise to consider your options carefully."

"Options," Isaac repeated, disdain creeping into his voice. "You speak of options as though I can choose from a selection of women like I'm picking fruit from a market stall. This isn't a game, Brisley. This is my life."

"And it will be even more difficult if you continue to resist the inevitability of it," Brisley pressed. "The King has been asking around about your matrimonial intentions. He expects you to make a decision soon."

Isaac felt a surge of frustration and helplessness wash over him. The King was concerned because if he picked the wrong woman tensions could lead to small feudal wars, as they had in the past, or in the least – trade between the counties could be affected. "What if I choose not to marry at all? What if I don't want to play this wretched game? I would rather remain single than be forced into a loveless union."

Brisley regarded him with a mixture of pity and concern. "That may not be an option you can afford. The pressure will only mount, and soon you may find yourself with little choice. You know how the court operates – perception is everything. You must appear to be the ideal Duke, not just in title but in action."

With that, Brisley turned and left the study, leaving Isaac alone with his thoughts. He stared out of the window at the sprawling gardens, the sunlight casting long shadows across the manicured lawn. His mind raced with possibilities, the weight of the world pressing down upon him.

In the quiet solitude of the room, he wondered about his future and the choices that lay ahead. Would he find a path that allowed him to remain true to himself, or would he be forced to conform like so many others chose? It couldn't be too distasteful, else it wouldn't even be an option. The thought of marrying for political gain was loathsome, but he couldn't shake the feeling that he was running out of time. He'd not even been the Duke that long, yet it felt like years had passed.

As the sun began to dip below the horizon, Isaac resolved to take charge of his own destiny somehow. He would not be a victim of the curse that haunted his family's history, nor subject to the whims of noble tradition. He would seek out a future that aligned with his own desires, whatever the cost. And as he turned back to his desk, his mind was set on the road ahead, free from the shackles of the past, at least for one brilliantly lucid moment.

It certainly had nothing to do with a familiar tune being hummed nor the familiar pattern of footsteps he could hear in the hall. He told himself that but wasn't too sure if he believed it.

Chapter Eleven

The morning sun cast a pale light over Langston Manor, struggling to pierce the layers of mist that clung to the gardens. There was a quietness to the estate that Isaac found unsettling, as though the manor itself was holding its breath, waiting for something – perhaps even him – to break the silence. The recent month or so had been marked by the heavy rituals of mourning and with them over, and the most of the mourners having left for their own homes once more it was as if even the walls were holding their breath, waiting to see what the new Duke would do next. And still, the title felt as burdensome as the dense fog that hung over the grounds.

Isaac had taken to wandering the gardens in the early morning hours before even most of the birds had awoken, seeking solitude in the maze of hedges and winding paths. He struggled to sleep anyway, and felt a bother to Williams. It felt a decent enough cure for his restless mind. Today was no different; he walked with hands clasped behind his back, his head bowed in thought, the weight of his family blood feeling almost tangible. He knew that a legacy had been passed to him, the greatness expected of him and, worse, the curse.

That curse had been the late Duke's singular obsession, he'd ascertained from the journals left behind, a fixation that had grown over the years, eating away at the man until there was almost nothing left. Isaac had witnessed his father's decline, even if from a distance, and the thought of ending up the same way left an icy dread in his heart.

The sun was truly up in the sky now, and he thought to head back in, but as he approached a corner of the gardens near the south terrace, he caught sight of Amelda, busily arranging a cluster of white lilies. She worked with a kind of quiet reverence, almost as if she were tending to something sacred. Amelda had been more present than anyone else, save Williams, since his father's passing.

Perhaps that was why he found himself approaching her now, his steps slowing as he drew near. She looked up, surprised to see him at such an hour, though her expression softened almost immediately.

"My lord," she greeted, setting down a pruning tool and inclining her head. "I trust you're well?"

Isaac let out a soft sigh, the question heavy with meaning. "Well enough, I suppose," he replied, though his tone held none of the assurance he would have liked.

He glanced at the flowers she had been arranging, the lilies stark against the dark green of the foliage. They were his mother's favourite flower, he realised with a pang. He recalled how much time she'd spent wandering these same paths as he, even in his brief recollections of her he imagined her only tatting lace and surrounded by the flowers. It was only in recent days that he'd come to understand why she might have found solace in them. The grounds were both beautiful, even surrounded by the mists, and undemanding of propriety. A rare place of peace.

"Your mother loved these flowers," Amelda said, almost as though she had read his thoughts. "Mrs Henderson told me that she used to work in the gardens when she was a lot younger, and that she had her plant them in the south gardens shortly after her marriage. I believe they're supposed to signify peace."

Isaac nodded slowly, the memory of his mother's laughter as she guided him through these very paths all those years ago flickering in his mind. He had been only six when she died, and yet the ache of her absence was as fresh as if it had happened yesterday. He remembered his father withdrawing further and further into himself after her passing, spiralling into a loneliness that had gradually hardened into bitterness.

"Do you think... people ever truly break free of their past?" he asked, surprising himself as much as her with the question. It wasn't the sort of thing he normally voiced aloud, but there was something about the stillness of the gardens and the presence of someone who seemed to understand him that made him feel as though he could speak his mind, if only for a moment.

Amelda regarded him with a thoughtful expression, her gaze steady and unflinching. "I believe people carry the past with them, my lord. But it doesn't have to define them. We can choose which parts to keep and which to let go."

Isaac considered her words, though they offered only a small comfort. "My father didn't see it that way. He let the curse define him, ruled his life by it, and in the end... it consumed him."

Amelda's expression grew sombre, though she remained silent. She, too, had seen the toll that the curse had taken on the late Duke, though she would never have spoken of it openly. He'd preferred the servants keep their distance from him after all. But the truth was evident to anyone who had spent time at Langston Manor: the curse, whether real or imagined, had haunted the family for generations, and the late Duke had allowed it to colour every aspect of his life, every decision he had made.

"It's a weight I can't seem to shake," Isaac admitted, his voice barely more than a whisper. "They want me to marry, to continue the Blackwood line. The King himself has written me on the matter. Even Lord Brisley decided to try to scold me on how I've yet to put forth my intentions to anyone. But how can I, knowing what lies in store?"

Amelda hesitated before answering, her gaze falling to the ground as if she, too, was wrestling with something unspoken. "Perhaps, my lord... perhaps the future need not mirror the past. I do not believe anyone is the sum of their blood. Their soul – that is entirely different."

The words hung between them, profound, and Isaac felt a small surge of hope rise within him, only to be quickly quelled by the gnawing doubt that had taken root since his father's passing. He wanted to believe that he could escape his family's fate, that he could make his own choices. But the curse was a constant presence, an unrelenting reminder of the price his ancestors had paid for their choices.

They walked in silence for a few moments, the gentle rustling of the leaves the only sound in the cool morning air. Isaac found himself drawn to speak again, the words tumbling out before he could stop them.

"I don't want to marry out of duty," he said, his voice raw. "I don't want to end up like my father, locked in a loveless marriage and then haunted by regret. Any student of history knows that the curse truly starts to enact revenge on my blood at such a time. But if I don't... the curse may still find a way to take its toll."

Amelda's expression softened, a flicker of sympathy in her eyes. "Perhaps... there is a middle ground, Your Grace. Perhaps you can find a way to honour the traditions you have to uphold without being bound by the, uh, curse."

Isaac let out a bitter laugh, though there was no humour in it. "And how, exactly, am I meant to do that? The very title of Duke is a chain, this blood that runs thick in my veins too, it is binding me to a tapestry that is woven half in myth and half in tragedy, and I fear that it is fixedly woven for the past, as much as it is my future."

Amelda was silent for a moment, as though weighing her response. "Perhaps... the future isn't as fixed as you fear."

Isaac glanced at her, a small flicker of curiosity stirring within him. "Do you truly believe that?"

She met his gaze, her expression resolute. "I believe we each have the power to shape our own destiny. Even if it is only in small ways."

He wanted to believe her, wanted to think that he could break free of the curse's hold and carve a path that was truly his own. But the fear remained, a dark, unshakeable presence that whispered of failure and doom. And yet, in that quiet moment, standing in the gardens with Amelda by his side, he felt a glimmer of something he hadn't felt in a long time: hope.

"Thank you, Amelda," he said quietly, his voice barely more than a whisper.

She inclined her head, a small smile softening her features. "You are welcome, my... Isaac."

As she turned to return to her duties, Isaac watched her go, a strange sense of peace settling over him. Perhaps he couldn't escape his family's legacy entirely, but perhaps, with the right choices and mind, he could do something that felt revolutionary.

For the first time since his father's death, he felt a small measure of control over his own fate, and as he stood there in the gardens, he allowed himself to believe that perhaps, just perhaps, he could find a way forward that was his alone.

The days in Langston Manor drifted by in a haze for Isaac, his mind consumed by the growing unease that had settled within him. Since his quiet morning in the gardens with Amelda, he'd felt ever more restless, and it refused to dissipate, as though a shadow was stirring within his thoughts, creeping into his sleep and clouding his mind. His nights had become a battleground, filled with vivid dreams that danced on the line between desire and dread.

It was always the same: he would find himself wandering the long, darkened hallways of Langston Manor, each room cloaked in shadow save for one, a faint light spilling from the doorway where Amelda sat alone, her gaze distant and sad. In these dreams, he felt his heart pounding with a strange mix of yearning and foreboding, as though drawn to her by a force beyond his control. Yet each time he reached out to her, a surge of dread filled him, thick and suffocating, a reminder of the family curse. His hand would drop, cold and empty, and he would stand there, trapped in the doorway, helpless and lost as he watched her face crack like a porcelain doll, her limbs falling to the ground.

Isaac would wake with a start, his heart racing and his skin slick with cold sweat, the lingering presence of Amelda still heavy in his thoughts. He tried to dismiss it as nothing more than a passing thought or the product of an overburdened mind. But the dreams continued, each one sharper and more visceral than the last, gnawing at his peace. It was as if something ancient and malevolent were weaving itself through his thoughts, stirring desires he hadn't dared consider and instilling in him a fear he was powerless to shake.

One evening, seeking answers or perhaps just a distraction, he sat alone in his study, pouring over an old journal his father had kept. The entries were filled with rambling thoughts, sketches of dark symbols, and ominous references to the curse. He'd studied not only history but the occult, religion, and any thing that might hold a snippet of fact or fiction that could comfort him or dispel the curse he so truly believed haunted him. There were mentions of dreams – his father's dreams – and cryptic notes about shadows that lurked within the manor walls. Each line was tense, written with a tremor that hinted at deep, creeping fear. His father's words seemed to echo in the quiet room, almost as if he were warning Isaac of the perils of love, of the dangers in ignoring the curse's demands.

"The curse feeds on love. It twists the heart's desires into weapons, turning fondness to torment and longing to ruin. A Blackwood is not free to love where his heart may lead."

Isaac's breath caught as he read, the weight of his father's obsessive dread settling heavily upon him. Could it be that his own dreams of Amelda were somehow entangled with this curse? The idea seemed absurd, yet he could not ignore the growing sense of dread that had rooted itself within him. He had seen what the curse had done to his father, how it had driven him to the edge, filling his mind with visions and shadows that seemed as real as the walls around them. Was he now following that same path, haunted by the same darkness that had plagued his father?

He closed the journal, his fingers trembling as he tried to banish the thoughts from his mind. But they lingered, gnawing at him like a dark parasite, filling him with the same terror he had seen in his father's eyes so many times before.

In the days that followed, Isaac attempted to go about his duties as usual, though the dreams and his father's words haunted him. He found himself searching for Amelda's face whenever she was near, though he kept his distance. Her presence seemed to stir both a strange comfort and a sharp pang of guilt, as though he were betraying some sacred boundary that was invoking those dark portents in his dreams.

But it wasn't only his own dreams that troubled him; there was a tangible tension between them now, a distance that had not been there before. He began to notice small changes in her manner, the way she averted her gaze when he was near, the stiffness in her posture whenever they passed each other in the hallways. The warmth he'd come to depend on in her presence was fading, replaced by a careful formality that felt like a wall between them.

He recalled the last time they had spoken in the gardens, the quiet understanding that had passed between them. But now, it seemed as though Amelda was withdrawing, retreating from whatever connection had been forming. It was as if she, too, sensed the darkness that lay between them, as though she were trying to distance herself from the shadow of the curse that had haunted his family for centuries.

The change unsettled him more than he cared to admit, and he found himself retreating to his study in an attempt to escape the turmoil within him. Yet his thoughts always circled back to Amelda, to her penetrating gaze and quiet understanding, the solace he had found in her presence even in his darkest moments.

One evening, as he sat alone with a glass of brandy in his study, he heard a faint knock at the door. Expecting Williams or one of the other servants, he called out, "Enter," without looking up. But when he raised his head, he found himself looking into Amelda's eyes, her face half-hidden in the shadow of the doorway.

"My lord," she said, her voice soft but steady. "I wanted to inform you that I'll be working in the east wing tomorrow. If you need anything, Williams will be in the study."

He nodded, though he felt reluctant to let her leave without saying something, anything to bridge the gap that had grown between them. The east wing was not a place many servants felt comfortable in, there were tales of a ghost that even Mrs Fletcher respected and feared. It was standard that the servants would report when they were assigned there so that they could be placed next in line for a leave to rest their nerves should they need it.

"Amelda," he said, his voice barely above a whisper. She paused, her hand resting on the door frame as she waited for him to continue.

For a moment, he considered telling her everything – the dreams, the longing in his heart, his fears about the curse, the way he felt as though he were losing himself to the same darkness that had consumed his father. But the words caught in his throat, and he found himself unable to voice the turmoil within him.

Instead, he managed only a weak, "Thank you, and take care."

Amelda inclined her head, her gaze flickering with an emotion he couldn't quite read before she turned and slipped quietly from the room.

As the door clicked shut behind her, Isaac let out a heavy sigh, feeling as though he had missed a chance to reach out, to find solace in her presence as he had before. But the fear of the curse, of dragging her into the darkness that had haunted his family, held him back. It was better this way, he told himself, better to keep his distance, to let her remain untouched by the shadows that clung to his life.

But as he sank back into his chair, he couldn't shake the feeling that he was losing something precious, something that might have offered him a path out of the darkness if only he had the courage to reach for it.

Over the next several days, Isaac's dreams grew darker, more intense, blurring the line between reality and nightmare. He would wake in the early hours, his heart racing and his mind filled with images of Amelda that remained imposed in the waking air, her face twisted in fear, her voice calling out to him in despair. It was as though the curse itself were taunting him, showing him what he could never have, tormenting him with visions of a future that could only end in ruin.

Williams would tend to him on those nights with the patience of a saint as he refused to ever voice his terror, offering a cool cloth, warm milk from the kitchen, and even sleeping herbs which he refused to touch lest he become trapped in his nightmares.

One morning, as he stood by the window in his study, staring out at the fog-laden gardens, he felt a wave of despair wash over him. The manor felt like a prison, the walls closing in as the weight of his cursed blood pressed down upon him. He could feel himself slipping, the same darkness that had claimed his father slowly consuming him. Isaac loathed the feeling of being so aware and yet so helpless against it.

And yet, despite everything, his thoughts always circled back to Amelda, not the vision of his dreams but the real woman that had offered him such kind words and comfort in her presence. He knew that he could not ignore the connection between them, nor the yearning that had taken root within his heart.

But he also knew that to pursue those feelings would be to invite disaster, to risk dragging her into the curse that had haunted his family for centuries. He could not condemn her to the same fate that had destroyed his parents' marriage, that had left his father a broken man consumed by bitterness and regret. Beyond that too, the chasm between them of their stations. He'd be unable to escape his title and she would find no welcome amongst his peers.

As the first light of dawn broke over the horizon, Isaac made a silent vow to keep his distance, to protect her from the darkness that had claimed his family. It was the only way to keep her safe, to ensure that she would not be touched by the curse that had already claimed so much.

And yet, even as he made the promise, he felt a hollow ache within him, a longing that refused to be silenced.

Chapter Twelve

The quiet of the east wing settled over Amelda like a heavy shroud. This part of Langston Manor was seldom used, and she had rarely been assigned duties here until recently. The grand but faded rooms, thick with dust and the scent of old wood, seemed to carry a strange energy, as if the echoes of long-past conversations and footsteps still lingered. Mrs Fletcher had assigned her to catalogue repairs, make note of which furniture needed mending or replacing, and to remove the carpets, beating them in the gardens to free them of dust.

The silence felt different here, not the kind that came from empty rooms, but the peculiar, charged kind that crept over her skin. Each step she took on the creaking wooden floors seemed to disturb the air, as though she were intruding on a space that had been left undisturbed for too long. There was a particular set of rooms at the end of the corridor that seemed darker somehow, the door sealed tight as if guarding something that would be better left hidden.

Her thoughts, half-formed and jittery, were interrupted when Clara appeared beside her, carrying the smaller of the carpets Mrs Fletcher had assigned them to. "Come along then, Melly," she said with a chuckle, though of the few outside her family Amelda let the fellow maid use the nickname on occasion as they'd grown close in the three years she'd served in the estate. "We'll finish beating these carpets in the garden, and I'll be glad to have the fresh air."

Grateful for the companionship, Amelda followed Clara through the back door and down the winding path that led to the quiet garden in the shadow of the east wing. Together, they stretched the carpet across the low rail, Amelda securing one end with a firm grip while Clara took up the old carpet-beater, her movements stronger than her small frame belied as she worked the dust from the thickly woven threads.

After a while, the rhythmic thuds grew louder, filling the quiet of the garden with the oddly satisfying sound and more dust than either expected. Clara, always quick to bring up her family, glanced at Amelda with a grin. "You know, my sister's off in the highlands now, tracking the nixies as they move with the seasons. She wrote me last week to tell me how she's finally got her book accepted for publication. I can hardly believe it!"

Amelda's eyes widened. "Truly? That's marvellous, Clara. You must be so proud of her. I didn't know she was writing a book on nixies – you gave me the impression that she only sketched water creatures. Ducks and the like."

"She did start with sketches," Clara explained, "but the more time she spent covered in Gods knows what muck – all the way up to her elbows, the more she started noticing the nixies, their habits, patterns, all the things the rest of us wouldn't give a thought to. It's taken her years, but she's travelled everywhere they go, she started here in Langston, she noted they're fond of mists, then followed them down near the river-lands, now of course – the highlands. She's marking their migratory patterns and all sorts of curious things. A proper naturalist she's become, I can bet she'll be accepted into the college of naturalists any day."

Amelda smiled, admiring the dedication that Clara's sister must have possessed to have observed the rare creatures for so long. Nixies, with their iridescent wings and fondness for avoiding humans, were notoriously hard to spot, let alone study. "It's a rare accomplishment," she said warmly. "There can't be many people in Briarvale who've tracked them so closely."

Clara's face glowed with pride, and she gave the carpet a particularly vigorous thwack. "Exactly what I told her. She's always had her head in the clouds, but now it's led to something worthwhile. When that book's printed, I'll be the first to buy a copy, and I'll tell everyone who will listen that I'm her sister." She chuckled, and her smile softened. "And the best part, Melly? Our family couldn't afford to put her through any schooling – she's done it all on her own. I think that's the most impressive part. She'll shake up those stiffs at the college."

As Clara continued, Amelda noticed a subtle chill prickling along her arms, a reminder of the strange feeling that had followed her since she'd entered the east wing. She glanced back at the manor's dark windows, half-expecting to see a shadow pass, but the glass remained empty. She was hesitant to call whatever the feeling was 'Duke Frederick' – but she wasn't going to avoid calling it that either.

"I can't imagine the courage it must take to go out to those far-off places," Amelda said, refocusing on the conversation. "She's lucky to have a sister who's so supportive, Clara."

"Oh, don't go flattering me too much," Clara said, laughing. "I nag her something dreadful whenever she returns, like a mother hen fussing over her chick, her hair looks a proper rat's nest when she comes back. She says I'm worse than our own mother for that."

Unable to shake the unnerving sensation from her time in the east wing, Amelda found herself wandering the dimly lit hallways that led toward the kitchen. The late hour had cast a hush over the household, save for the occasional flicker of candlelight that painted shadows against the walls. Sleep had evaded her, the faint stirrings of her earlier work lingering on her mind and unsettling her in ways she couldn't quite articulate. Perhaps a momentary diversion in the warmth of the kitchen, she reasoned, might steady her.

As she entered, she was surprised to see the head butler, Williams, standing by the stovetop with a pot of milk simmering gently. He looked up as she stepped inside, his normally impassive face softening in acknowledgement.

"Couldn't sleep, Miss Amelda?" he asked, his voice a low murmur that somehow suited the quiet of the kitchen.

"No," she admitted, offering a faint smile. "The east wing, I suppose—it felt… strange to work in that part of the manor." She paused, glancing at the pot of milk. "Are you also having trouble with rest?"

Williams sighed, shaking his head as he carefully stirred the pot. "His Grace has had a restless few nights, to say the least. Thought a bit of warm milk might soothe his mind." He paused, his gaze thoughtful. "It's been a difficult period for him. Understandably so, given the responsibilities he's had to assume so quickly."

Amelda frowned, concern welling in her chest. "I hadn't realised. Has he been having nightmares?"

Williams seemed to hesitate, as though weighing how much to share. "Yes," he said slowly, keeping his voice low. "Night terrors, if you will. He tries to manage it on his own, not wanting the staff to notice, but…" He trailed off, the faint creases in his brow betraying his own worry. "It's unlike him to show much vulnerability. His father was the same way as you know."

Amelda nodded, understanding all too well how the late Duke had always shielded his troubles behind a wall of stoicism. "Is it the grief, perhaps?" she asked carefully. "Losing his father so recently…"

"Grief can twist the mind in strange ways," Williams replied. "But I suspect there's more to it than that. His father – Augustus Blackwood, may he rest in peace – had his own struggles with… night-time torments. A great deal of distress plagued him, and I can't help but think that perhaps young Master Isaac has inherited more than just the title."

The mention of the late Duke's name caused a chill to settle in the air. Mrs Fletcher had often spoken, in hushed tones, of Augustus's peculiar moods, his unyielding sense of dread that he never seemed able to shake. The staff had long whispered about the Blackwood curse, though few dared to discuss it too openly in the presence of the family.

Williams cleared his throat, as if breaking his own trance. "Now, I don't believe much in curses," he said with a sharp, sensible tone, though Amelda could see the shadow of uncertainty in his eyes. "But the human mind is a powerful thing. If someone believes themselves cursed, they'll find the very thing they fear wherever they look. I've seen it before."

"Then you think it's only belief?" Amelda asked, seeking reassurance.

"That would be the reasonable explanation," he said with a nod, though he didn't look quite as assured as his words. "Augustus believed he was marked by some ancient spite, and he built his life around that fear. If the young Duke were to simply disregard it, perhaps he could free himself from such nonsense."

Amelda watched him quietly, absorbing his words. She could hear the note of caution beneath his pragmatism, a silent appeal for discretion. "If he needs support… well, he doesn't have to face it alone."

Williams glanced at her, his eyes kind but thoughtful. "Miss Amelda, you have a good heart, and I daresay His Grace knows it. But you'd do well to remember that a man's troubles are sometimes best kept within the confines of his own mind. Still," he added, with a gentler tone, "it may be of some comfort to him to know that others are willing to shoulder the burden, should he ever wish it."

As the pot of milk finally began to bubble softly, Williams removed it from the heat and poured it carefully into a small porcelain cup. "Goodnight, I hope you find rest as well too. You're coming back to the main house soon I hope?"

Amelda nodded as the butler left and took a moment to herself to organise her thoughts. She'd tried to maintain a little more distance from Isaac before she'd been called to serve in the east wing. She knew how improper their friendship alone could be, and her heart ached to close that gap each time they spoke.

She tried to tell herself that there should be no harm in being close to the Duke, but her heart and mind were at a war where she had no idea who the victor might be.

The following morning, Amelda felt an undeniable sense of lightness as she made her way back to the main house, her duties in the eastern wing finally complete. As she entered the laundry room, the familiar scents of soap and fresh linens enveloped her like a comforting embrace. There was an undeniable solace in the tasks of washing and pressing, each fold of fabric erasing the uneasy memories of the east wing's looming shadows. They required little thought themselves, and let her mind wander back to whatever books she was digesting in the moment.

Mrs Fletcher was already in the laundry room, frowning over a stack of sheets in need of mending. She looked up when Amelda entered, her face a mixture of relief and exasperation. "There you are, Amelda. I've been meaning to have a word with you about the state of that place." She shook her head, almost muttering to herself as she lifted the linens. "The east wing's gone to seed, it has. More work needed than I'd imagined. Why, it'll cost a small fortune to see it made right again."

Amelda nodded, sharing in her exasperation. "It's worse than I thought too, Mrs Fletcher. I noted cracks in the plaster, and some of the floorboards are warped. Even the furniture is beyond simple repair."

Mrs Fletcher huffed. "I'll need to bring in some labourers to quote the cost of repairs – hopefully sturdy men not prone to feeling the unease the east wing gives one – there's only so much we can do ourselves. The Duke ought to be made aware, of course, but I'll not trouble him with figures until I have something solid. With all he's handling at the moment, I'd rather not add to his burdens." She paused, softening as she looked at Amelda. "He's a good man, the young Duke, but under more strain than he'll let on. The estate's maintenance is hardly something he ought to concern himself with just now."

Amelda sensed the tension in Mrs Fletcher's words, feeling again the weight of what Isaac was enduring, but she simply nodded. "You're right, Mrs Fletcher. I'll finish preparing the list of what needs replacing in the meantime." She offered a faint smile, eager to return to the simpler, familiar tasks of the laundry. "It's good to be back here, where things feel... more settled."

Mrs Fletcher raised an eyebrow, catching her meaning. "Aye, I'd say you're not the only one who feels that way. I myself wouldn't spend another day in the east wing unless I had to. Gives me the shivers, truth be told."

Relieved by the solidarity, Amelda allowed herself a small laugh, glancing around the laundry room at the steam from the hot irons and the comforting piles of linens, folded and waiting. "It's as though the whole atmosphere changes as soon as you leave that side of the manor."

Mrs Fletcher chuckled as well, wiping her hands on her apron. "Well, you're back now, and just in time. There's a mountain of work here that's far better suited to you. The irons are warmed, and I dare say these sheets won't fold themselves."

Chapter Thirteen

The storm struck Langston Manor with a force unlike any Isaac could remember, shaking the old walls and battering the windows with rain so heavy it seemed to drown out even the thunder that roared above. The wind howled around the manor, rattling doors and carrying with it an almost feral quality, a raw energy that felt as though it could tear the very roof from the building. Lightning flashed outside, illuminating the ancient portraits on the walls and casting shadows that danced in the firelight, unsettling and restless. There was a distinct sense that nature itself was bearing down on the manor, intent on ripping away whatever secrets or darkness lay within.

Isaac paced his study, watching as the storm raged against the night. His mind was a tempest in its own right, unsettled and brooding as he fought against the emotions that had been swelling within him over the past weeks. Dreams, visions, and fragments of his father's writings swirled together in his thoughts, conjuring a deep and abiding fear. But beneath that fear, perhaps even stoking it, was an undeniable draw toward the one person who had, unknowingly or not, come to haunt his every thought.

It was nearly midnight when a knock sounded at his study door. Isaac turned abruptly, blinking as he composed himself. He half-expected Williams, his butler, there to check on him after a flash of lightning had sent a rumble throughout the house. But when he opened the door, he found Amelda standing there, her expression composed yet touched with a quiet intensity that sent a thrill through him.

"Amelda," he said, surprised but unable to hide the warmth in his tone. "I hadn't expected anyone to be wandering the halls at this hour, given the storm."

She gave a small nod, stepping just over the threshold but keeping a respectable distance. "Forgive me, Your Grace, but I came to ensure you were all right. The storm's already caused some damage in the east wing, it's lucky no repairs have been started. Still, I wanted to be certain it hadn't troubled you."

Isaac's heart stirred at the kindness behind her words, and recalled her relocation to the east wing itself, how terrified she must be too, though he forced himself to remain guarded. "Thank you, Amelda," he replied, his voice quieter now. "It's good to know someone has sense enough to look after the rest of us." He paused, his eyes lingering on her halo of red hair that deepened to brunette in the shadows. She was like a steady light amid his uncertainty, the calm in a storm he could neither control nor escape.

The storm surged again, sending a powerful gust of wind that rattled the windows. Amelda glanced toward them before returning her gaze to Isaac, her eyes searched his even as a crack of thunder vibrated through the room. In that moment, the low lamplight framed her face in soft shadow, and he couldn't stop himself from feeling how deeply he wanted – needed – her presence.

"Amelda," he began, his voice barely above a whisper. "You…you've no idea how much your company has meant to me of late. I fear I've kept too much of myself shut away. If it hadn't been for you…" He trailed off, unsure of how to voice the sentiment without revealing too much of the state of his mind. But his words had lingered, and her eyes softened, even as she maintained her composure.

"You have been through much," she replied gently. "No one could fault you for finding solace where you can." Her gaze was calm, thoughtful, yet there was something behind it – something she, too, was keeping carefully guarded. "It's only natural that you'd turn to others, given the burden you carry."

Isaac drew in a breath, searching her face for some sign that she felt the same draw, the same tension that had plagued him. And there it was, in the slight tremor of her hands, in the way her gaze held his for a moment longer than was proper. A dangerous, undeniable current seemed to spark between them, something they had both perhaps felt but never acknowledged.

"Amelda," he said, the restraint in his voice finally slipping. "I don't think you know how much…how much strength I find in you. How much I've come to rely on your presence here, in this house, despite everything." His words tumbled out before he could stop them, spilling over like the rain outside. "You bring a peace to this place that I've never known – one I certainly don't deserve."

A flicker of something – hurt or confusion, perhaps – crossed her face, and she took a small step back, though her gaze never left his. "My lord, you are kind, but…" She paused, drawing in a steadying breath. "You must remember who you are. And who I am."

Her voice was quiet, all but drowned out by the storm and tinged with sadness. She turned her face away, as though distancing herself would make her words less painful to deliver. "I am only a servant. It would do neither of us any good to… blur those lines. There is no place for admiration of this sort between us."

Isaac's heart sank, but he pressed on, determined to make her understand. He felt like he was rambling, the floodgates were open. "I know all too well what divides us," he said, his tone earnest. "I know what's expected of me, the life that's been laid out for me since birth. But that doesn't change how I feel." He hesitated, wondering if he had already gone too far. Yet the intensity in her gaze spurred him on. "You are a constant in a world that feels as though it's falling apart. I cannot – will not – simply pretend that you mean nothing to me."

Amelda's hand twitched as though she wanted to reach out to him, but she restrained herself. "I know, Isa – Your Grace. And that's why you must resist. You and I both know what would happen were you to step outside the bounds of what's accepted."

She stepped back, as if retreating from the dangerous territory they had stumbled into. "Please, don't let your heart lead you into ruin, my lord. I beg of you, for both our sakes."

Isaac felt the sting of her words, but he could not deny their truth. His father had warned him of the dangers of letting emotion dictate his life, of allowing the heart to guide him where this curse forbade. He had witnessed the ruin it had brought upon his father, the bitterness that had hollowed him out, leaving him a shadow of the man he had once been. And yet, standing here in the flickering light, watching Amelda struggle with her own emotions, Isaac felt his heart rebelling against the chains that had bound him all his life.

Thunder crashed outside, shaking the walls, and Amelda's gaze flickered back to him, her expression tense and torn. She seemed to be wrestling with her own inner conflict, her loyalty to her position clashing with something deeper, something unspoken.

"Amelda," he said softly, taking a step closer, "I won't ask for anything more than you can give. I know our positions, our lives... they're worlds apart. But I hope that I can still rely on you, that I can still find some comfort in your presence." His voice was low, almost pleading. "You have become more to me than a servant."

She held his gaze, her expression unreadable, but he could see the emotion flickering in her eyes, the weight of what was unsaid heavy between them. Finally, she drew in a deep breath, as though steeling herself. "My lord, I will always be here to serve you," she said quietly, though her words felt more like a dismissal than a promise. "But we must both remember our places, and what is best for both of us."

A flash of lightning illuminated the room, casting strange shadows across her face, and for a brief moment, Isaac thought he saw a flicker of pain in her eyes. But as quickly as it had appeared, it was gone, replaced by the calm, professional demeanour she wore like armour.

"I understand," he said, his voice barely audible. "Forgive me for speaking so freely."

She gave a small nod, acknowledging his apology without meeting his grey eyes. "There's no need to apologise, my lord," she replied softly. "We both know the strain you've been under, the burdens you carry. But I urge you to keep yourself whole, sane – this, I fear it is neither. I should not have come, I should have let Williams tend to you tonight. Perhaps I lost my head."

Isaac nodded, swallowing the lump that had formed in his throat. She was right, of course; it was nonsensical to want for this connection they shared to flourish into more. But as he watched her turn to leave, he couldn't shake the ache in his chest, the feeling that he was losing something precious, something he had perhaps never truly had.

As the door closed softly behind her, he felt the weight of his loneliness settle over him once more. The storm continued to rage outside, its fury matched only by the turmoil within his own heart. He knew what was expected of him, the life he was meant to live. But tonight, as he sat alone in the flickering firelight, he could not help but wonder if he was doomed to follow the same path as his father, to live a life bound by duty and tortured by this damnable curse, bereft of the one thing that might bring him peace.

The hours slipped away in the dark solitude of Isaac's study. As the storm outside pounded against the walls of Langston Manor, a different kind of storm roiled within him. His thoughts kept returning to his father, to the man's grim, distant demeanour and the coldness that had seeped through every part of his life. Since his father's passing, Isaac had rarely allowed himself to dwell on the pain of those memories. But tonight, alone with only the weight of his own heart, he could no longer hold back the flood.

The late Duke had lived a life guided by duty and haunted by regret, a life which Isaac was now beginning to recognise as a cautionary tale he'd perhaps been too young to understand at the time. When Isaac was a boy, his father had ruled the household like a figure carved from stone: stern, silent, and isolated even from his family. The distance had grown deeper as Isaac reached adolescence, and the Duke's fixation on the family curse became more than just a tale to frighten children – it became an all-consuming obsession. He'd spent hours reading and re-reading family records, sequestering himself away in the study, convinced the curse held the answers to the failings he felt had plagued the Blackwoods for generations.

Isaac remembered vividly the long, tense silences at the family table, the way his father's eyes would drift over his mother's empty seat without a hint of warmth. Theirs had been a marriage of political necessity rather than love, arranged in the time-honoured tradition of preserving lineage and securing alliances. Yet whatever ambitions the Duke's marriage had achieved, between that and her death, it had left little room for any familial love.

Once, as a young boy, not long after the funeral, he had asked his father outright why he and his mother rarely spent time together. The Duke's face had darkened, and he had replied simply, "Love is a folly for men without obligations, Isaac. You'll understand that when you're older." It was a conversation Isaac had never forgotten, and it had weighed on him for years, carving out an ever-widening divide between his own yearnings and the life he was supposed to lead.

Isaac took a deep breath, willing himself to shake off the memories, but they only gathered strength as his mind drifted back to the lingering presence of Amelda, the way she had looked at him tonight with so much fear, so much patience, and he must have imagined the longing being returned to him. Her words had been intended as caution, but they had set something ablaze within him.

Did he truly want to walk the same path? To marry for duty, to live in loveless detachment, and to suffer the silent despair that had hollowed out his father?

He pushed himself to his feet, pacing the study as his thoughts grew louder, more insistent. His father had believed the curse to be more than a myth; he had claimed that every Blackwood who denied the family's fate would be doomed just the same. It was as though the family were bound by invisible chains, locked into lives of isolation and dread. His father had even recorded his own thoughts on the curse in a series of disjointed notes and entries, each feeling like a descent into madness he too would follow.

One of those entries came to him now, as vividly as if he were reading it from the very page:

"To love is to open oneself to the possibility of ruin, of suffering, of failure. The curse does not forgive such recklessness. It waits, watches, and strikes at the heart. I have come to accept that some things are best left in the realm of caution, for any Blackwood who risks defying his fate will find himself met only with despair."

Isaac had always found the entry troubling, and at the time he read it, he hadn't understood the depth of his father's bitterness. He had dismissed it as the product of a man scarred by too many years spent in isolation, of a man who had surrendered too much of himself to the darkness.

But now, with Amelda's voice still lingering in his mind, Isaac felt himself standing at that very crossroads. Was he truly prepared to endure a lifetime in which love was an impossibility, a mere folly? Could he willingly consign himself to a life void of companionship to guard himself against more pain than could be tolerated?

He'd not attended his father's deathbed, and his letter delivered by the way of his solicitor offered more warmth than he'd given in life, yet even then, there was no peace, no forgiveness, no release. It was as though he had taken every unspoken resentment, every unfulfilled dream, with him to the grave.

The firelight flickered, casting shadows along the shelves of his father's journals and letters, each page chronicling a life of guarded obedience to a legacy Isaac no longer fully believed in. He took down one of the journals, flipping through it to a passage he recalled from memory. The handwriting was spidery and difficult to read, but the words etched themselves into his mind:

"We live not for ourselves but for those who came before us. To deviate is to invite ruin; to love is to invite suffering. There can be no exceptions."

Isaac closed the journal, setting it back on the shelf with a sense of finality. His father had lived by these words, and he had suffered for it. Isaac's jaw tightened as he stared at the worn leather spines, feeling as though the room itself were closing in around him, the walls pressing down with the weight of Blackwood blood.

The house, the estate, the title – he had inherited it all. But he knew now that he had also inherited a choice: to live as his father had, bound by fear, or to find his own path, to choose a life of meaning, regardless of the curse that may or may not linger in the shadows.

He thought again of Amelda, of the warmth in her voice, the quiet understanding in her eyes. She had reminded him of his obligations, yes, but she had also stirred something in him he could no longer deny – a resolve to live on his own terms, even if it meant embracing the possibility of heartache.

In that moment, Isaac felt a kind of clarity settle over him, like the eye of the storm. The curse, if it truly existed, thrived on fear, on resignation, it latched into their hearts regardless. His choice was between a curse and the aching regret of not living, or small snatched happiness before he was consumed. He thought of his father's warning: "The curse does not forgive such recklessness." And yet, would it not be reckless to deny himself joy?

The storm continued to rage, the wind howling against the manor, rattling the windows as though urging him to make his decision. Isaac straightened, feeling the weight of his father's life slipping from his shoulders, leaving only a quiet determination in its wake. He did not have all the answers, and he knew the path ahead would be fraught with challenges. But as he stood there, gazing at the fire, he felt for the first time in his life that he was ready to forge a life of his own, to shape his own destiny.

Isaac turned his back on the study, leaving his father's journals untouched on the shelves. He would carry his father's memory as a warning, but he would no longer allow it to dictate his choices, his heart. And as he left the room, the storm began to subside, as though granting him permission to step into the unknown.

Chapter Fourteen

Under a grey morning sky, Isaac strolled the grounds, his mood contemplative. Despite his recent resolution to walk his own path and defy the blood in his veins, the whispers about the family curse had begun to invade his thoughts again. His mind drifted to the mounting expectations surrounding him, both spoken and unspoken. He knew what the household expected of him – to marry swiftly, to secure the Blackwood lineage, and to settle into the role of a noble with heirs and alliances. He was sure he'd seen Mrs Fletcher asking Williams about clearing out his mother's rooms for the future Lady Blackwood. But now, with every new morning, Isaac felt less and less inclined to conform to that destiny.

His route took him past the grand fountain at the centre of the manor's gravelled courtyard, where statues of Blackwood ancestors loomed. These statues, brought over centuries ago from the far off kingdom of Destein to the south across the seas, had always struck Isaac as unnervingly lifelike, as though his ancestors' spirits were trapped within the stone. Today, with his mind preoccupied, he barely glanced at them. His steps slowed as he heard the crunch of gravel, and he looked down at his boots.

As he lifted his gaze, he felt a subtle but sudden sensation, as though the air around him had shifted. A faint rumble grew behind him, louder and more ominous by the second.

He turned, and in the instant he recognised the threat, he had barely time to react.

The statue closest to him – a towering marble likeness of a stern-faced Blackwood ancestor he couldn't begin to name – began to lean forward, its stone base shifting on the uneven gravel. With a harsh scraping sound, it tipped, as if it were some ancient spectre lunging for him, its arms rigid and cage-like.

Isaac barely managed to take a step backward before the statue struck him. The heavy stone collided with his shoulder, forcing him down and pinning him against the gravel. The weight of it drove the breath from his lungs, and for a terrifying moment, all he could hear was the throbbing of his own pulse, his vision blurring as he tried to focus on his surroundings.

A strangled yell tore from his throat, and though he struggled to wriggle free, he was trapped by the immense weight of the statue pressing on his leg. Gravel bit into his back, his trousers tore, and a sharp pain shot up his calf, but it was the weight – the terrible, unyielding weight – that made his mind whirl with panic.

The sound of approaching footsteps echoed across the courtyard, and then came Williams's voice, sharp and anxious. "Your Grace! Hold on!"

After what felt an eternity crushed by the literal remnants of his family, Williams, Mr Gatrell, and the gamekeeper, Mr Cropp, reached him. Faces tight with concern, they scrambled to assess the situation, casting hurried glances between each other as they realised the extent of what they had to lift.

"On the count of three, then," said Williams, his voice low and steady, though Isaac could see the strain in his brow. He may have not been a young man, but he was certainly as fit as one. "We must lift it enough for him to get his leg out – anything less, and we risk the statue falling back again."

Isaac clenched his teeth as they positioned themselves, bracing to heave the statue back even as his muscles trembled with tension. As the three men counted aloud, Isaac felt the statue shift slightly. Gravel scraped beneath him, and with a swift tug, he managed to wrench his leg free just as the men pushed the statue upright again, leaving it teetering unsteadily before it resettled with a thud.

Isaac lay back, gasping for air, while Williams knelt beside him, immediately inspecting his leg. "Only bruised, it appears, but we can have a physician look over it," he murmured, though his tone betrayed his unease. "Your Grace, you were incredibly fortunate."

Shakily, Isaac pushed himself upright, feeling the smarting ache where the statue had pressed down on him. His leg bore a nasty bruise, but miraculously, nothing seemed broken.

"Thank you, all of you," Isaac managed, his voice barely above a whisper. He was still processing the enormity of what had just occurred. The statue's sudden fall, as if it had been tipped by unseen hands, played over and over in his mind.

"Perhaps we should consult a builder or stonemason about the stability of these statues," Gatrell suggested, his tone as calm as ever, though his eyes carried an unspoken warning. "It would be best to ensure none of the others are similarly unsteady."

"Yes... yes, of course," Isaac murmured, though he knew well enough that the statue had stood unmoved for centuries. Even as a child he'd played near it without a second thought.

As he made his way back toward the manor, he noticed the tense glances exchanged between Mr Gatrell and Cropp. They, like many of the other servants, were already whispering about the curse. And as Isaac reached the doors of the manor, he heard a soft murmur from one of the passing maids.

"Seems the curse is restless. First the branch, and now the statue..."

Isaac quickened his pace despite the pain, feeling an uncomfortable prickle on the back of his neck.

Upstairs, Amelda worked quietly in the library, attempting to focus on her duties as she dusted the shelves and arranged books in their proper order. Yet her thoughts had drifted, her mind preoccupied with the journal she had found hidden among the Blackwood records. The journal had been written by a Blackwood ancestor, detailing his heartbreak after forsaking a love affair for a political marriage. The ancestor's former lover had cursed him and his descendants, vowing they would suffer as he had. And it was this journal that she now kept hidden up in the attic, for she couldn't shake the feeling that it held answers Isaac needed to know.

But what good could come from sharing this knowledge with him? Would it help him or only deepen his fears? She had wrestled with the decision for days, the weight of the secret pressing on her even as her loyalty to Isaac urged her to confide in him.

Lost in thought, she nearly jumped when she heard voices in the corridor outside. She froze, straining to listen, recognising the familiar tones of the housemaids as they passed by.

"Another accident," one of them whispered. "This time, nearly crushed by one of those statues in the courtyard. It's as if the curse has taken a more violent turn."

Amelda's heart dropped. She knew of the fallen branch from a few weeks ago, which had narrowly missed Isaac, but now this? A chill ran through her as she imagined the statue toppling down, nearly crushing him. She felt an urgency rising within her, a need to speak with Isaac, to warn him of what she'd read.

The knowledge from the journal haunted her. According to its pages, the curse was exacted upon those who burned too hot in pursuit of duty. While she'd tried to tell him that he was more than his duty – and could forge his own path, it felt as if fate knew that he was bound to fall upon his sword for that duty. The curse would not merely stand by, idle, when such inclinations appeared again within the family line. But who could have imagined it would manifest in such a physical way? A falling branch, a statue... it seemed too coincidental to be anything but a sinister sign.

She turned away, gripping the duster in her hands, her knuckles white. She had tried to brush off the curse as a superstition, a relic of a bygone era meant to frighten children, but now she found herself doubting even more. What if the curse had a mind of its own? What if it was truly becoming more aggressive, perceiving Isaac's reluctance to fulfil the role expected of him and to do more to have a legacy of his own will?

The following morning, Isaac sat in his study, his leg sore and his thoughts burdened. The statue incident had disturbed him deeply, more so than he had let on to Williams or the others. He knew, or hoped, they all attributed the mishap to some forgotten instability in the stone, but Isaac couldn't dismiss the sense of intent behind it. It was as though the statue's fall had been orchestrated, a deliberate warning aimed directly at him.

He caught sight of his own reflection in the study's glass cabinet, and the weariness in his own eyes surprised him. He'd always scoffed at the idea of a curse; his father's fervent belief in it had struck him as an unnecessary paranoia, a kind of madness he'd hoped to avoid. But now, his thoughts circled uncomfortably around his father's last days – days spent in obsessive worry over the curse and the noble duty to marry well, to avoid any risk of defying their place according to the journals.

A gentle knock at the door broke him from his reverie, and Williams entered, radiating a calm he envied. He paused, watching Isaac closely, and Isaac couldn't help but notice the shadow of concern in the butler's eyes.

"Your Grace," Williams began, his voice carefully measured, "I wonder if I might speak frankly."

"Of course," Isaac replied, gesturing for him to continue.

"Some of the staff have become quite unsettled," Williams said, folding his hands as he spoke. "With two incidents occurring so close together... well, there's talk of the curse again. They believe that perhaps it is asserting itself in response to..." he trailed off delicately, as though reluctant to broach the next part.

"In response to my hesitation to marry, I know the stories around the curse," Isaac finished for him, a grim smile tugging at his lips. "Damned from inheritance of title until marriage or damned after it. I even checked the history books myself. The peace my grandparents had… my grandmother did not know that before marriage. She lost how many siblings before my great-uncle abdicated?"

Williams nodded slowly. "Yes, Your Grace. They fear that the curse has taken note, and that it is becoming... insistent."

Isaac gave a heavy sigh, feeling the bitter taste of the conversation settle over him. He realised that Williams, ever loyal and respectful, had likely known of the curse and it's intricacies for years, standing silently by as Isaac's father had grown increasingly neurotic. The butler's steady gaze held no judgement, only an unspoken support.

"Williams," Isaac said quietly, "do you believe in this curse?"

Williams hesitated. "I believe," he said carefully, "that the Blackwoods have carried a heavy burden for many generations. And I believe that your father's adherence to that burden – however it may have troubled him – was rooted in a genuine fear of what might befall him otherwise."

A silence hung between them, each understanding the implications without needing further explanation. Isaac rose, feeling the resolve he had forged during the storm begin to flicker under the weight of these reminders.

As he looked out the window, his thoughts turned once again to Amelda. She alone, of everyone in brought him some clarity of purpose that he otherwise failed to grasp. Yet he could sense her own reservations, a reticence that suggested she too was burdened with secrets.

The time had come, he realised, to confront the truths he'd long avoided. Whether the curse was real or not, and what his course of action must be. He would have to make a choice, one way or another, before the curse made it for him.

Isaac found himself drawn to the library more and more often lately, a quiet sanctuary where he could momentarily shut out the noise of duty and expectation. He'd learned his father was fond of the room and as much as he loathed to follow in his footsteps, he was determined to figure his mind out.

Today, a grey light filtered through the large windows, and the scent of paper hung thick in the air – a blessed dichotomy to the hum of speculation from the household staff about the curse. He pretended not to hear, yet he could not tell his ears not to listen.

He moved along the shelves aimlessly, letting his gaze brush the titles along the spines of books he'd likely never read, his thoughts consumed by the latest incident with the statue. The sense of foreboding that had taken hold in the last week was gnawing at him, a reminder more solid than his bruise, of his father's obsession with the family curse. Isaac resisted the pull of that same paranoia, but it was becoming more difficult with each unnerving accident, each whispered comment from the servants.

The library door creaked open, and he turned to see Amelda entering quietly, a cloth in hand as she continued her morning duties. She hadn't noticed him at first, her focus directed at a shelf in need of dusting, but when she lifted her gaze and saw him standing there, a moment of surprise passed over her face before she schooled it away.

"My apologies, Your Grace," she murmured, dipping her head slightly. "I didn't mean to intrude."

"No intrusion, Amelda," he replied softly. "In fact, I… I welcome the company."

A tentative silence settled between them as she resumed her task, her movements practiced and familiar. For a moment, Isaac simply observed her, allowing the calmness of her presence to ease his mind. It was in these stolen moments that he felt a measure of peace, a reprieve from the weight he carried.

After a few minutes, Isaac found himself compelled to speak, voicing the thoughts he'd kept hidden for too long. "Amelda, have you ever wondered…" He hesitated, uncertain of how much he could confide. "About this so-called curse?"

She paused, her cloth still poised over a row of books, and turned to meet his gaze. He could see the hint of something unreadable in her eyes, a flicker of understanding, as though she, too, was haunted by the family's dark legacy.

"I suppose I have," she replied cautiously, her tone soft. "It's difficult not to, given all that's happened."

Isaac nodded, letting his guard slip for a moment. "I keep telling myself that it's mere superstition, a relic of my father's mind – but then…" He trailed off, his thoughts circling around the strange series of incidents that had shaken his belief. "How many accidents can one man endure before he starts to doubt his own scepticism?"

Amelda's eyes softened, and she looked at him with a sympathy that caught him off guard. "Sometimes," she said, choosing her words with care, "we hold onto rationality because it's all we have against fear. But I think even the most sensible among us… can sense when something larger is at work."

Her words hung between them, unspoken fears given life. For the first time, Isaac felt as though he had found someone who understood, someone who didn't dismiss his worries or interpret them as weakness. He searched her face, realising with a startling clarity how deeply he valued her presence in his life.

"Amelda," he murmured, the words coming unbidden, "you've been… an anchor for me. Amidst all of this uncertainty, you are the one thing that makes sense."

She looked away, a faint blush colouring her cheeks, but she did not withdraw. Instead, she clasped her hands together, gathering her composure before speaking again. "Your Grace, I… it is not my place, but I cannot bear to see you troubled."

Her words were laced with genuine concern, and Isaac felt his heart tighten. Without thinking, he stepped closer, his hand lifting as though to bridge the invisible gap between them. For a heartbeat, his fingers hovered near hers, a touch so close yet forbidden. When she didn't recoil, he let his fingertips brush the back of her hand, and dared let his fingers lace in hers. Her hand was so much colder than his own, and he longed for the moment to last longer.

The touch was brief, almost too brief, yet it felt as though something profound had passed between them in that single moment. A connection neither of them could deny, though both knew the implications were fraught with risk.

Amelda withdrew her hand slowly, her gaze lowered. "Your Grace... Isaac," she whispered, the intimacy of his name on her lips both exhilarating and terrifying, "you mustn't do this. We cannot... not like this."

Her voice trembled with a mix of restraint and longing, and Isaac's heart twisted at the sight of her inner struggle as much as he delighted to know his feelings might be reciprocated. He realised, with painful clarity, that his feelings for her were no longer mere gratitude or companionship; they were deeper, sharper, and entirely ungovernable. He was falling for her.

"Forgive me," he murmured, though he couldn't bring himself to regret the moment. "It's selfish of me, I know. I don't wish to burden you with... these feelings. But you are the only one I feel I can be honest with, Amelda."

She looked up at him, a raw honesty in her expression. "And you are the only one I can speak to in kind," she replied, her voice barely above a whisper.

A silence followed, the cloak of their shared confession pressing down on them both. Isaac knew the impossibility of what he was admitting, but in that moment, all he could see was the woman standing before him, her mere presence a balm to his troubled soul.

Eventually, she spoke, her voice firm but tinged with sadness. "Your Grace, whatever... whatever we may feel, you are bound to your duty, and I to mine. We cannot risk... scandal or harm to either of us."

He nodded, though the resignation in her words struck him like a blow. Duty, the very concept that had tormented him for as long as he could remember, had once again drawn a line between what he wanted and what he could have.

"Of course," he said quietly, stepping back, the space between them once more insurmountable. "You are right, Amelda. I would never wish to bring harm to you, or to see you suffer for my... for my feelings."

A heavy silence lingered as he turned away, feeling the sting of his own restraint. He understood the boundaries that separated them, yet in his heart, he couldn't deny the sense of destiny that had brought her into his life.

As he reached the door, he looked back at her, one final glance before he forced himself to leave. Her expression was unreadable, but her eyes held a sadness that mirrored his own.

When he left the library, the sense of loss settled over him, heavy and all-encompassing. He knew that, in time, he would be forced to face his family's legacy, to choose between the curse's unyielding hold and his own desire for happiness. And yet, the thought of a future devoid of Amelda's presence filled him with an emptiness he couldn't ignore.

As he walked down the hallway, Isaac felt as though he was standing on the edge of a precipice, the weight of his future pressing down upon him. There was no easy path forward, only the knowledge that whatever he chose, it would shape the course of his life – and perhaps hers – forever.

Chapter Fifteen

The morning dawned dull and cold, as though even the sun was reluctant to rise on what Isaac knew would be another day of reckonings he would rather avoid. Autumn threatened to bludgeon what little sunshine Langston received, and he could feel it pressing on with the same finality of a ticking clock. He had come to dread the small but mounting pressures – family obligations, the murmurs of the servants, and his own thoughts, which oscillated wildly between the fleeting moments of solace he found with Amelda and the encroaching demands of his position.

When Williams entered his study carrying a letter bearing the royal seal, Isaac's heart sank. He forced himself to remain impassive, but the subtle gleam in Williams' eyes betrayed his own understanding of what such a letter meant. Though outwardly composed, Isaac felt the weight of his responsibilities settle even more heavily on his shoulders.

"Your Grace," Williams said quietly, extending the envelope to him. "A message from His Majesty."

Isaac's hand lingered for a moment, reluctant, before he accepted the letter and dismissed Williams. Alone, he broke the seal and unfolded the letter with a sense of foreboding.

My dear Duke of Blackwood,

I trust this letter finds you well, even amidst the many trials that accompany the inheritance of such an esteemed title. Allow me, however, to remind you of a duty as pressing as it is personal. It is the Briarvale tradition to marry within a year of inheriting the title, securing the family line and ensuring the continuance of one's noble legacy.

I would expect that, given your father's own dedication to our shared ideals, you understand the necessity of this duty. Indeed, the preservation of the Blackwood estate requires that you marry suitably, choosing from among the most esteemed houses of the realm.

I have every confidence that you will handle this matter with the same commitment and dignity that befits your name.

Yours faithfully,

Henry R.

Isaac's hands tightened around the letter as he set it down on his desk, the weight of the King's reminder heavy on his mind. It was not a simple, idle expectation; it was a command, shrouded in the polite wording of royal correspondence, yet clear enough to leave no room for doubt. His heart sank further as he read the letter again, each word reminding him that his desires were irrelevant in the face of such obligations.

In truth, he had been delaying the inevitable for as long as he could. He'd found excuses for every invitation, every introduction to some eligible young woman with which a distant family friend, or indeed, family such as Lord Brisley extended in letter. But now, with this particular letter in hand, he knew he could delay no longer. It wasn't simply a matter of familial expectation; it was a matter of duty to the crown and country, a demand that would only grow louder until it was fulfilled.

Isaac sank into his chair, pressing his fingers to his temples, his mind racing. Marriage – he had always known it would be a requirement of his station. But he had not been prepared for the finality of it, the realisation that once he stepped onto this path, there would be no turning back. And the thought of entering into a loveless union, driven by duty and tradition alone, filled him with a bitterness he could scarcely describe.

As he sat in silence, the flicker of his feelings for Amelda intruded on his thoughts, a brief respite amidst the dark clouds gathering in his mind. Their moments together had been few as of late, and tinged with the bittersweet reminder that neither could cross the boundaries drawn between them by birth, but they had somehow managed to illuminate the dreary landscape of his life. Her presence had become a balm, a place of comfort he had never expected to find amidst the isolation of his role.

But he knew that these feelings, however deep and sincere, were as futile as they were dangerous. His title and status could offer her nothing but hardship if he dared to cross that line, and he could only imagine the scandal it would provoke. Not only would it destroy her reputation and safety, but it would also draw the ire of the King himself, a betrayal of both loyalty and duty.

The thought of letting her go, of severing the fragile connection between them, felt almost unbearable. But was it not the only sensible path forward? He could not jeopardise her life, her standing, merely for the fleeting comfort her presence offered him.

As the day wore on, Isaac found himself pacing the study, consumed by indecision. His thoughts swayed between longing and resignation, a mental tug-of-war he knew he could not maintain. When Williams returned with more correspondence later in the afternoon, Isaac addressed him, his voice weary.

"Williams, have you any insight on… these matters?" he asked, gesturing to the royal letter still resting on his desk. "It seems as though the King has sent a gentle but firm reminder of my… obligations."

Williams, ever the discreet confidant, regarded him with a poised gaze. "If I may be frank, Your Grace, it is a position many of your rank have faced. But it is also true that those who pursued such alliances purely for duty often found themselves trapped, not only in loveless marriages but in lives of quiet misery."

Isaac nodded, appreciating Williams' honesty. The butler had served the family for years, had watched his father sink into despair and obsession, watched his parents be shackled by a marriage that had wrought nothing but loneliness even before death. The man was even old enough to have served his grandparents and their seemingly blessed union.

"But the King's words," Isaac said, his voice strained, "leave little room for choice, don't they?"

"Perhaps, Your Grace," Williams acknowledged, "but choice does exist in the way you fulfil your obligations. Happiness may be elusive in a union made for duty, but it is not impossible. The difficulty lies in finding someone who, even in such an arrangement, might offer companionship... even contentment."

Isaac knew Williams was right, but the hope of finding someone who might understand him, someone with whom he could share even a fraction of the connection he felt with Amelda, seemed impossibly small.

Later that evening, as darkness fell and the household settled, Isaac once again found himself alone in the library. The shelves, filled with stories and histories, seemed to mock him now, reminders of the countless Blackwoods who had come before him, bound by the same expectations that now threatened to imprison him.

His mind drifted to Amelda – her musical laughter, her eyes which mirrored his own thoughts back at him. It was as though she had slipped into his life at the very moment he needed her most, offering him solace amidst the storm of his inheritance. And yet, the more he felt for her, the further she seemed to slip from his grasp, her very existence a reminder of the impossible choice he faced.

The flickering candlelight cast shadows across the room, and Isaac realised he was no longer alone with his thoughts. The curse, that lingering shadow his father had been so consumed by, seemed almost palpable now, as though it were waiting, watching, for him to make a misstep.

If he chose duty, he would secure the duchy in his family, continue the line, and fulfil the King's expectations. But if he chose his heart, he would face ruin – not only for himself but also for Amelda. And in that ruin, the curse would find its hold on him, binding him to a fate as dark as his father's. While he was sure his official heir, which he'd affirmed would be his cousin Theodore, would be capable of the administration of Langston itself – he found he did not lack a heart in that he'd inflict the cruelty of the curse that afflicted the current Duke or Duchess.

He rose from his chair, feeling the suffocating weight of his decision bearing down on him. There were no easy answers, no clear path that would offer both duty and happiness, and he knew that whatever choice he made, it would alter the course of his life irreversibly.

As he left the library, tired of continuing to search for answers, Isaac felt a chill pass through him, a premonition of the battles yet to come – both with the curse and within his own heart. He only hoped that, when the time came to choose, he would have the strength to bear the consequences.

Amelda sat alone in her small, dim room, the flickering candlelight casting wavering shadows across the journal spread open on her lap. She'd secret it back into the alcove of the attic soon enough, but for now she allowed her curiosity to run rampant. Each page had unfolded another part of the Blackwood family's troubled past, a legacy of betrayal, heartbreak, and vengeance. She had read through the journal in snatches over the past few nights, the words of the ancient scorned lover revealing a curse that was far darker and more deeply entrenched than even the household rumours suggested. Tonight, however, she'd found a hidden slip of paper that had fallen out from between the leather cover and the hinge, the last page of the journal that had come unglued with age.

It was not written in the same hand, but the penmanship of another. This alone was enough to give her pause.

It was a warning, penned by a woman whose words spoke of sorrow and rage so old it seemed to bleed through the pages. The original Duke Blackwood, it said, had made an irrevocable choice. He had been betrothed to a woman of high standing to fortify his family's position and power, yet his heart had belonged to another – an alchemist's daughter from the nearby village, a woman he had loved with a depth he had concealed until it was too late. This she'd already read in his own hand of course. His ambition and fear of losing his legacy had driven him to cast her aside, as well as an unborn child which he claimed could not be his. This – she had not known. And in that act of betrayal, a curse had been born, uttered by the woman he had wronged.

The lover's words resounded in Amelda's mind as though they were spoken directly to her. The curse's power, the fuel by which this mystic woman sank into the Blackwood blood, did not stem from that single act of betrayal alone, but from a cycle of repression, a history of Blackwoods choosing duty over love, and the curse fed upon it as a ravenous carrion bird. The passage she read now held the key to ending the Blackwood family's torment – only by a true act of love, a choice made not from duty but from genuine, unbidden feeling, could the curse be broken, and it must be broken anew with each generation lest it continue to fester in the Blackwood blood 'til the curse has starved and no more will the choice ever be considered.

Amelda felt her pulse quicken as she closed the journal and the hidden passage from the woman who struck the curse itself, resting her hands on its worn leather cover. She had always known the Blackwood legacy held a darker burden, one that had gripped the late Duke and now pressed upon Isaac. His father had been consumed by it, his melancholy and paranoia deepening over the years until they had shaped the cold, distant man everyone remembered. Amelda had seen glimpses of the same burden in Isaac's gaze, but it was only now, with the full knowledge of the curse, that she understood its relentlessness.

But that was not all. The curse was not simply a passive presence, waiting for yet another generation of Blackwoods to fall under its weight. It thrived on denial, on rejection of true feeling. Amelda's heart twisted as she thought of her own quiet affections for Isaac, the connection she felt was undeniably deepening with each moment they shared. This was something she had never intended or foreseen, yet it felt as inevitable as the rise and fall of the sun. And with that feeling, a darker realisation settled upon her: the curse might already be stirring, sensing the conflict in Isaac's heart and interpreting their connection as a threat.

She shivered as she recalled the recent accidents – the falling branch that had nearly struck Isaac, the statue that had pinned him, leaving him miraculously unscathed save a bruise, and of course, the night terrors she'd heard whispered about by fellow servants. At first, she had hoped them mere coincidence, but now the sequence of events felt deliberate. The curse, if she allowed herself to believe in it's existence, was rearing up, reacting to his uncertainty. The more he denied his heart, the more it seemed the curse tightened its grip.

Amelda's hands trembled as she closed the journal and carefully returned it to its hiding place, making sure not a trace of her reading was visible. If Isaac discovered that she had unearthed the family's secrets, it would lead to questions she wasn't prepared to answer. She took a slow breath, letting her gaze drift over the room, collecting herself. There was no one to turn to with this knowledge, no confidante to help her shoulder this burden, and she knew she would have to make her own choice. She had no idea if telling Isaac would corrupt any answers he sought to end his torment.

To protect Isaac, to spare him the slow descent into misery his father had endured, she would have to let him go. Or rather, she would have to push him away, severing whatever was beginning to blossom between them. A dull ache settled in her chest at the thought. Though she would never confess it aloud, these past months had awakened feelings within her she had long since abandoned as foolishness. She had known it was dangerous to grow close to Isaac, yet a part of her had believed their connection could remain innocent – a mere friendship, a source of comfort in his otherwise lonely life.

But the truth was painfully clear now. It was no longer safe for either of them to indulge in these stolen moments, these soft words exchanged in quiet rooms or caught in the gardens where the skies held no judgement on the blood they'd been born into. By sharing even these small confidences, they were only stoking the flames of the curse's wrath. And if she was right, if the curse was indeed stirring in reaction to his feelings, she could not allow it to escalate. She would have to break the bond between them before it grew into something neither of them could survive.

She knew of his duty, and he could find love within it if he allowed his heart to open to it. But not while she remained.

The heartache of that decision weighed heavily upon her. How would she bear it, knowing he would never truly understand why she was distancing herself? How would she find the strength to turn away from the one person who had, for the first time, made her feel truly seen?

Yet she knew there was no other choice. The fate of the Blackwoods – and perhaps her own – rested on this sacrifice. Isaac's destiny had to remain untethered to her, free to find another, someone he could genuinely love untainted without the danger of a curse waiting in the wings to claim him.

That night, Amelda lay awake in her bed, staring into the darkness, preparing herself for the inevitable. She would end this properly. She would harden her heart and do what was necessary. It would hurt them both, of that she was certain, but it would protect him. And to Amelda, there could be no higher duty than protecting Isaac – even if it meant sacrificing her own happiness in the process.

Chapter Sixteen

Isaac stood by the grand window in his study, gazing out at the spreading grounds of Blackwood Manor, feeling a tightening in his chest that was becoming all too familiar. The accidents – the tree branch, the statue – had shaken him, and he could no longer deny the spectre of the Blackwood curse looming over him. It wasn't just in the incidents themselves but in the way they seemed to strike precisely at moments when his mind wandered to Amelda. The curse had plagued his father and countless other Blackwoods before him, preying on each generation's weaknesses, and it was not so far-fetched as to think it might exact a terrible price from him for the connection growing between them.

He closed his eyes, and she was there, vivid against the dark, every detail of her, her voice, the quiet courage she carried, her soft laughter that had brought such light into the lonely halls of Langston. He was sure it was the curse – the curse or his own folly – making these feelings burn as fiercely as they did. Though their friendship remained pure, he had caught himself in moments when he dared imagine more, even dared ask for more than he deserved. Each time his heart drifted towards her, something happened that brought him back to the grim reality of his life and the fate of his family. He was haunted, and he could not allow her to fall victim to that same fate.

The answer seemed clear, if brutal. He would put an end to their time together, their conversations, and all the subtle moments that had come to mean so much to him. His only solution was to immerse himself in his duties, pouring his energies into managing the vast estate, meeting with tenants, inspecting the lands, and overseeing affairs that could only be handled by a Blackwood.

Across the manor, Amelda was making her own painful decisions. She, too, was aware of the dangers, though her understanding was drawn from a different source. The truth of the curse lay heavy on her heart. She could not help but wonder if her presence, her very feelings for Isaac, were stirring the darkness that plagued his family. With every stolen glance and unspoken thought, she felt herself tempting fate, jeopardising his safety, and stoking the anger of a curse that would not rest until it had claimed its next victim.

She knocked quietly on Williams's door, and he greeted her with the reserved warmth of a man who had long grown accustomed to her presence in the manor. His steady gaze, the way he always seemed to know more than he let on, made her uneasy today, and she shifted under his scrutinising look.

"Williams, might I ask you a favour?" she asked, her voice barely a whisper.

The old butler nodded. "Of course, Miss Amelda. How may I be of assistance?"

She hesitated, unsure how to phrase her request without exposing her true intentions. "I… I fear I've been lax in my duties of late. I was caught reading in the library yesterday, and –" she paused, glancing at his face to gauge his reaction, "—and I thought it right I be reprimanded. Perhaps, if you mentioned it to Mrs Henderson, or Mrs Fletcher… they might assign me some extra duties."

Williams's eyes narrowed slightly, but his expression betrayed nothing. "Indeed, Miss Amelda. The cook, I'm certain, could use the extra hand. You have my word; I shall inform her discreetly." He dipped his head, though she did not miss the knowing glint in his eye. He was not blind; he had surely witnessed the burgeoning friendship between her and Isaac and could likely sense the unspoken attachment that lay beneath.

"Thank you, Williams," she managed, her voice faltering. She turned to leave, feeling the weight of her decision settle heavily on her shoulders. This was for the best; it had to be.

Williams watched her retreating figure, his brows knitted together in thought. He knew that there was more to Amelda's request than she was letting on, yet he would keep her secret, for he knew the weight such secrets could carry. Amelda had been a loyal servant at Blackwood, even through the late Duke's most troubled years, and she deserved the trust she had earned.

Over the following days, life at Blackwood Manor fell into a quieter, more relentless rhythm. Isaac was scarcely seen outside his duties, absorbed entirely in his work, dealing with accounts and the management of the estate's far-reaching affairs. Each morning, he left early to inspect the grounds or meet with tenants. He greeted them with polite attentiveness, though a touch of his usual warmth was missing. Every duty he performed was coloured by the mounting dread in his heart, his mind repeatedly drifting back to Amelda, no matter how sternly he reprimanded himself. The weight of his resolve felt heavy and cold, and he began to feel as if he were slowly erasing parts of himself he had cherished.

It was the same for Amelda. Each day she reported to the kitchen, where Mrs Henderson wasted no time in assigning her the most tedious and time-consuming of tasks. She scrubbed pots, polished the silverware, sorted the pantry, and hauled firewood for the ovens until her fingers were sore, her eyes crossed from tiredness, and her back ached. But this was exactly what she had wanted, and she was determined to endure it. With her mind occupied by endless chores, there was no time to dwell on what might have been. She kept herself out of sight, always just beyond Isaac's reach, retreating when she heard his familiar tread. It was a silent, invisible dance of avoidance, but one that she clung to, convinced it was the best way to keep him safe.

One afternoon, Isaac was in the courtyard, receiving a group of tenants who had come to discuss concerns about the recent harsh weather and its impact on their crops. Amelda, lugging a sack of firewood back to the kitchen, paused as she caught sight of him across the yard. She stood at a distance, the heavy sack weighing down her arms, watching as he listened intently to the farmers, his brow furrowed in concentration. She could see the lines of worry etched into his face, the haunted look in his eyes that had grown more pronounced with each passing day.

It broke her heart to see him like this. Isaac had always been kind, with a warmth and humour that set him apart from the typical aloofness of the nobility. Now, he looked more like a man bearing the weight of generations on his shoulders, haunted by a legacy he had inherited unwillingly. The dreams she had kept hidden – dreams of a life where they could speak openly, laugh freely, share moments that were not restrained by the accident of their births – felt as distant and unattainable as ever. She turned away, blinking back the sting of tears. She could not afford to dwell on fantasies that could never come to pass.

Yet that night, sleep eluded her. Alone in her tiny room, she lay awake, her thoughts drifting once again to Isaac, wondering if he, too, was lost in the shadows of the past, haunted by memories he could not escape. She allowed herself to imagine, for one brief, reckless moment, a life in which she was not a servant, and he was not the Duke. They would walk together beneath the stars, laugh over cups of tea, share their dreams and burdens without fear of consequence. But that life was not hers to claim, and she knew she must bury such thoughts if she were ever to find peace.

For Isaac, the long hours of work and the endless cycle of duties offered little respite. Though he spent his days focused on the practicalities of running an estate, his nights were another matter. In sleep, he could not escape the visions that haunted him, memories of Amelda slipping into his dreams like smoke, impossible to grasp yet painfully vivid.

In these dreams, she was beside him, her laughter like a balm to the ache in his heart. He would reach for her, only to feel her slip away, dissolving like the mist that clung to Langston. Other nights, the dreams were darker; he would see her in danger, ensnared by the very shadows that plagued his family, calling his name as he tried to reach her. He would wake in a cold sweat, his heart pounding, his mind racing with fear. Each time he thought of her, the curse felt closer, as if it had taken notice of his thoughts, poised to punish him for daring to want so fiercely.

By day, he reminded himself of his duty. He reminded himself that he was the Duke, with responsibilities that went far beyond his own desires. And yet, in the quiet moments, when he was alone in his study or walking the silent halls of the manor, he could feel her presence lingering in his mind, a part of him he could not let go.

Each night, as Amelda sat in her room, letting exhaustion pull her into a restless sleep, and each day, as Isaac buried himself in his work, they both carried the weight of unspoken words, silent longings, and the knowledge that their lives were bound by a duty neither could escape. And in the stillness of those quiet hours, when the world was dark and empty, they each wondered if there was, perhaps, another path. A life where they could be free from the weight of the past, where love could flourish without fear.

But dawn would break, and they would resume their roles, bound by duty, haunted by dreams, and divided by the unyielding walls of Langston Manor.

The morning autumnal mist clung to the grounds as Isaac strolled along the garden path, his mind lost in a battle between reason and feeling. The conversations he had replayed over and over in his head all converged on one truth: he had to make a decision, and soon. The King's letter was still tucked in his desk drawer, though its words echoed in his mind, pressing him with the weight of his duty. He had resolved to sever the one bond that had begun to mean everything to him, for it was the only way to secure the Blackwood legacy. As if fate were mocking him, he spotted Amelda emerging from the side path that ran by the rose garden.

Their eyes met, and Isaac felt the surge of everything he had been attempting to silence within himself. For a moment, he considered retreating, sparing them both the pain, but he forced himself forward, reminding himself that this was the right course, and that it was for her protection as much as his.

"Amelda," he said, his voice more unsteady than he had intended.

She gave a slight smile and dipped her head respectfully. "Your Grace." She rarely addressed him so formally, and hearing it now only made his resolve feel all the more cold and unnatural.

There was a long pause before he spoke, as if saying it aloud would make it real. "I intend to marry, Amelda. A lady of good standing, as… as is required. I haven't anyone in mind yet, but… I wanted you to know."

The words fell like stones between them, and she blinked, the hurt flashing in her eyes, though her face remained calm. "Of course," she replied quietly, her voice devoid of bitterness but tinged with sadness. "It is your duty, after all."

Isaac's throat tightened as he studied her, standing so still, so quiet, the grace of her presence somehow giving him strength and stealing it away all at once. "I didn't want you to think…" he began, trailing off as he found himself unable to finish the thought. He didn't want her to think he was callous or unfeeling, that he had simply cast her aside as if their friendship and their mounting feelings had meant nothing. But he couldn't find the words, couldn't explain the storm of emotions he felt without risking more pain for them both.

Amelda nodded slowly, each motion careful, as though she were holding herself together by sheer will. "I understand, Your Grace. Truly. It was bound to be this way, and it's for the best. You... you have a legacy to secure."

He felt as though she had driven a dagger into him with her simple acceptance. The bond between them – one that had grown so quietly yet powerfully over the months – was severing before his eyes, and it felt as though he were losing part of himself in the process.

"I hope you'll find happiness," she added, her voice softer than before, almost like a whisper carried on the wind. "You deserve that, and... maybe even to break this curse."

Isaac could only nod, barely trusting his voice. "Thank you, Amelda. For everything." He fought to keep his composure, to hold himself as the Duke he was meant to be, yet he couldn't shake the hollow ache settling in his chest.

As she turned to go, she hesitated, glancing back at him once more. "Your Grace, may I... may I request leave for a week?" Her voice was formal again, restrained. "To visit my family?"

A slight wave of relief washed over him at her words; she needed distance, just as he did. He nodded. "Of course. Take all the time you need."

With a last respectful dip of her head, Amelda turned and walked away, her figure retreating down the gravel path, leaving Isaac to wrestle with the choice he'd made. The rose garden was quiet, save for the rustling leaves, but it felt as if the very air had grown heavier, mists thicker, pressing down on him with the knowledge that he'd taken a step he could never undo.

Amelda arrived at her family's cottage late that evening, her heart both weary and relieved as she approached the place she had once called home. The comforting smell of wood smoke greeted her as she stepped inside, where her mother, a tall woman who had shrunk in her age, was mending a shirt by candlelight, just as Amelda remembered her doing countless times in her childhood.

"Mother!" she said warmly, and her mother looked up, a surprised smile breaking across her face as she rose to embrace her.

"Oh, Melly! I didn't know you were coming," her mother said, squeezing her tightly. "You look fit to be wrung after a wash. Are they working you too hard over there at Langston?"

Amelda managed a slight smile as she set down her small travel bag and removed her shawl. "It's not so bad. But I needed to come home. Just for a while."

Her mother's eyes softened as she ushered her to the table, where another half-sewn shirt lay draped over the chair.

"It's good to see you, dear. I'll put on some tea, and you can tell me all about your work."

Amelda smiled but shook her head gently. "I'd rather hear about you, Mother. How have things been?"

"Oh, we manage," her mother replied, her tone cheerful despite the modesty of their surroundings. "Your sister's expecting her first. She and Nelson are over the moon – he's already making a cradle for the little one." Her voice was filled with a pride, and Amelda felt a pang of happiness mixed with envy. Her elder sister had found happiness, a love unburdened by impossible barriers, a life she could never hope for.

They chatted late into the evening, and Amelda listened intently as her mother spoke of her sister's preparations for the baby, of the neighbours' news, small gossip she'd overheard. It felt grounding to be here, far from the grandeur and turmoil of Blackwood Manor.

Just as the kettle began to whistle, her younger brother, Edwin, returned from work, his cheeks flushed from the cold as he stepped inside. "Melly!" he called out, his face lighting up when he saw her.

"Edwin," she replied, pulling him into a hug. He had grown since she'd last seen him, his shoulders broader, his hair longer. In her mind's eye, he had been little more than a boy, and now he was on the cusp of manhood though she saw him last just as summer started for Mary's wedding.

He grinned as he set down his bag and loosened his scarf. "You're just in time, you know. I'm making your favourite for dinner, you certainly do have a lot of luck, seeing as I didn't know you were coming. You don't visit us near enough either."

She smiled, feeling a warmth she had not felt in weeks. "Well, it's good to see you too, Edwin. Please don't feel the need to nag though."

"Nonsense," he said, rolling up his sleeves with a theatrical sigh. "It's what younger brothers are for. Besides, I've nearly finished my apprenticeship. Soon I'll be a proper smith, and I won't be home much longer to nag, I should get my fill."

Amelda's chest swelled with pride. "Then we'll celebrate tonight. For you, for Mary and her little one, do you know if she's visiting soon?"

They spent the evening cooking together, talking about Edwin's apprenticeship, her sister's growing family, and her mother's small sewing business. As they sat together over the meal, a sense of peace settled over Amelda, something she had sorely missed amidst the dark corridors and haunted memories of Langston Manor. Here, she was not troubled by curses nor her foolish heart; she was simply Melly, slotting neatly back into her family home.

Later that night, she lay awake in her childhood bed, staring at the ceiling and listening to the sounds of the night. Her mother's quiet breathing from the next room, the occasional creak of the house settling, and the distant bark of a dog were all reminders of a life she could have chosen if she'd chosen differently, found work in the village. Yet thoughts of Isaac crept into her mind unbidden, memories of his haunted face, his heavy silences. In the safe haven of her family's cottage, she found herself, again, wishing for something she could never have, longing for a world in which love and duty could coexist.

For now, she could only hope that he would find peace and that perhaps, in some way, she had helped him toward it. But as sleep claimed her, she knew that no matter how hard she tried, her heart would always carry the quiet ache for the impossible.

Chapter Seventeen

The morning of Isaac's departure from Langston Manor arrived cloaked in a thick mist, lending a cold and heavy stillness to the grounds. The Manor, usually imposing, now seemed to recede into the fog, as if reluctant to release him. His decision to travel to the capital had been a resolute one, borne from a sense of duty and the need to escape the ever-present shadows of Langston and the weight of his own growing emotions. Yet, as he waited for Williams to finish loading his luggage into the carriage, an odd sense of foreboding lingered in his chest.

"Everything is prepared, Your Grace," Williams informed him, giving a curt nod as he secured the last of the trunks.

"Thank you, Williams," Isaac replied, his voice softer than he intended. Forcing himself to adopt a more determined tone, he took a final glance back at the Manor. "Let's be on our way."

The journey was a calculated effort to find a suitable bride, someone noble, refined, and poised – a woman who could assume the role of Lady Blackwood without the complications of emotion. He had convinced himself it was the only choice left, a necessary step in preserving the family name as he ought to, and, perhaps, avoiding the curse that had shaped his father's life.

Yet, as the carriage trundled through the countryside, each mile taking him further from the world he knew, Isaac found it difficult to silence the thoughts of what he was leaving behind. The memory of his last encounter with Amelda replayed in his mind more than he cared to admit. Her acceptance, her quiet sadness – it had felt as though he had torn away a part of himself along with the bond they had shared. The very purpose of this journey was to seek freedom from that connection, and yet, the further he went, the more the separation seemed to consume him.

The first half of the journey was uneventful, with the mist gradually giving way to grey skies and the familiar autumnal gloom. Williams sat opposite Isaac in the carriage, occasionally glancing over to check on his master, though he refrained from any attempts at conversation. He could see the strain in Isaac's expression, a silent turmoil that the Duke seemed determined to endure alone. Williams knew better than to pry, yet he couldn't ignore the quiet desolation that seemed to have settled over the young man.

They reached the outskirts of a small village just before dusk, and Isaac, weary from travel and pensive from his inner thoughts, suggested they press on rather than stopping to rest. Williams offered no objection, his loyalty unbroken despite his own thoughts on the matter. But as the carriage rumbled down a narrow road cutting through a dense patch of woods, the first rumbles of thunder sounded overhead, and the dark clouds released a sudden torrent of rain.

The horses grew restless, the rain pelting their backs as the wind picked up, bending tree branches in sweeping arcs that scraped the sides of the carriage. The driver whipped the horses onward, urging them to quicken their pace, but just as they reached a bend in the road, a deep crack sounded through the air – a branch, heavy and sodden with rain, splintered and fell across the path. The horses reared, their hooves flailing, and the carriage veered sharply.

Isaac barely had time to brace himself as the entire vehicle lurched and tilted, a sickening jolt shuddering through his bones as it rolled onto its side. The sound of shattering wood and splintering glass filled his ears, his body thrown harshly against the carriage wall. For a brief, terrifying moment, the world spun, and everything went black.

When he opened his eyes, Isaac found himself half-buried in debris, his vision blurred as he struggled to make sense of his surroundings. His head throbbed, and a sharp pain radiated from his shoulder, but through the haze of confusion, he could feel the cold rain soaking through him, he recognised the sight of Williams bending over him, his face etched with concern.

"Your Grace – are you all right? Can you hear me?" Williams' voice was calm, steady, though Isaac could see the barely concealed panic in his eyes.

"I… I think so," Isaac managed, his voice hoarse. He tried to shift, but the pain flared, forcing a grimace. "What happened?"

"The carriage overturned," Williams replied, carefully assisting Isaac to sit up as his body protested. "A branch fell across the path, and the driver lost control. We were fortunate – could have been much worse."

Isaac nodded faintly, though his mind was not at ease. There was a strange, lingering sense of dread that went beyond the shock of the accident. The curse crept back into his thoughts. The Blackwoods, cursed with misfortune and misery should they betray what they should stand for… His own father had been consumed by fear and dread, withdrawing into a world of isolation and ritual, and Isaac had always vowed he would not allow himself to follow that path. But the notion of the curse was beginning to feel far less distant and far more real with every beat of his heart.

He glanced at the remnants of the carriage, its splintered wood and broken wheels strewn across the road. The near miss felt like more than mere misfortune; it was as though fate itself were taunting him, reminding him of the stakes he faced. Each decision seemed suddenly perilous, each step in his path fraught with unseen dangers. If he were to marry for duty alone, as his father had done, would he not be condemning himself to the same fate, to a life shadowed by emptiness and dread?

He took a deep breath, steadying himself as Williams helped him to his feet. The driver, unharmed but shaken, awaited them a few yards away where he'd tethered the horses to a fencepost. They seemed calmed despite everything, and he approached clutching his hat nervously.

"Begging your pardon, Your Grace, but there's little hope for the carriage," he said, his voice apologetic. "Nearest town I know to have a physician's a fair few miles away and I doubt nary be awake. I can still fetch help if you'd like?"

Isaac waved him off. "No need. We'll manage." He looked to Williams, whose presence lent him an unexpected strength. "Help me gather my things. We'll return to Langston Manor."

"Return?" Williams echoed, surprised. "But I thought you meant to journey on to the capital? Besides, your injuries –"

Isaac hesitated, a storm brewing in his gaze. "There are… matters that need attending to at home. I'll not risk any more misfortune on this path. Not tonight. The horses are well enough to carry us home?"

The driver nodded with a curt "Aye."

"Then see to it they're saddled even if you have to use our clothes."

Though he didn't voice it aloud, he knew that returning to Langston, to the estate would only deepen the whispers that would swirl around the family curse. The strange accidents, the creeping sense of danger – they were all warnings, and he could no longer afford to ignore them.

By the time Isaac and Williams returned to Langston Manor, the skies had cleared, though the memory of the storm lingered in Isaac's mind like a dark omen. He settled himself into his study that very night while Williams protested that he should rest while a physician was fetched. He lit a single candle and stared at the pile of journals, letters, and old family records that lay before him on the desk. Some were familiar; others were volumes he had never dared explore, believing they held no more than the fancies of ancestors long gone. Now, however, he felt compelled to uncover whatever knowledge might be hidden within those pages.

As he sifted through the dusty records, he found himself drawn to a particular journal belonging to his great-grandfather. The handwriting was faint, nearly illegible, but the entries spoke of similar worries – a strange illness, dreams that seemed to bear sinister warnings, and visions of loss and despair. It became clear that his great-grandfather, to no surprise, had been haunted by the family curse, and the tone of his words grew increasingly frantic as he recounted the years spent grappling with the mysterious forces plaguing the Blackwood name.

One passage struck Isaac with particular force:

"The curse binds us, all for the price of a heart betrayed. A choice made in earnest can break it, they say… yet none have dared to test its bounds. What then of those who love in secret, their true hearts hidden beneath duty and pride? Must they, too, suffer the curse's wrath?"

The words resonated with Isaac, echoing the very struggle he now faced. He felt trapped between duty and desire, burdened by a choice that seemed as perilous as it was inevitable. The story of his father, a man consumed by fear, and his great-grandfather, who had spent years searching for a remedy to an ancient curse, were stories he now feared might become his own. Yet he was also certain that love, the one force that might stand against the curse, was the very thing they, and he, had chosen to forsake. Betwixt the two of his cursed forebears, was his grandmother and grandfather. There were stories he knew of, their great love despite all that had come about before them. He felt so assuredly that it must be the key with which they'd lived lives of relative peace.

By dawn, the study was strewn with papers, half-read letters, and fragments of folklore that only served to deepen his unease. There were countless theories and superstitions, vague accounts of spirits and curses, yet nothing concrete, nothing that could offer him a way forward besides his own theories.

As he slumped back in his chair, weary and frustrated, he allowed himself to close his eyes for a moment, Amelda's face flashing into his mind's eye. He saw her standing in the garden, her gaze steady, her presence a balm against his own fears. But he knew that no matter how much solace she brought him, no matter how deeply he cared, he could never voice the truth. The curse, he realised, would turn any admission of love into a sentence, binding him to the same fate his father had endured.

Isaac rose painfully from his chair and stood by the window, gazing out over the darkened grounds of Langston Manor. He felt the weight of generations bearing down on him, the memories of his father, his trials, his fears. Somewhere beyond the veil of time, he imagined the first Duke Blackwood, the man who had summoned the curse, watching, waiting to see whether he too would fall victim to the same fate.

With a final glance back at the journals strewn across his desk, Isaac made a silent vow. If he were to break the curse, he would do so by action, following the one answer his forebears had not: the courage to choose, even against everything he'd come to know was proper.

As Amelda lingered by the market stalls in the village, she revelled in the simplicity of her surroundings – the fragrant herbs, the warm fug of freshly baked bread that quaked against the autumn air, and the pealing laughter of the local children darting between vendors. These small, precious moments reminded her of a life untethered by the duties and tensions that governed Langston Manor. Her week away had been restorative, providing her a fleeting sense of freedom and a return to her family and village friends, who had long been absent from her daily life.

Yet, even in this simplicity, her mind constantly returned to the estate, and more specifically, to the Duke she had left behind. She couldn't shake the image of Isaac's cheerless face as he told her of his plans to marry. Their parting had left a sunken ache in her chest that nothing seemed to fill, and as much as she'd tried to focus on her mother and siblings, the thoughts of him lingered, persistent as the changing of the seasons.

As she was about to move on from a vendor's stall, her attention was drawn to an elderly man who shuffled toward her. His clothes were dark, his gait slow, yet his face bore an unmistakable familiarity. She squinted, recognising him faintly as one of the estate's older servants, though his name escaped her. He wore an expression of quiet urgency, his eyes fixed on her with an intensity that cut through the gentle hum of the market.

"Miss Amelda," he murmured, voice lowered so only she could hear. "I have something for you. From Langston."

The mention of the estate immediately piqued her interest, though a familiar sense of caution rose within her. "What is it?"

He handed her a small, neatly folded letter, its edges creased as though it had been carried a long way. "I've done what I must, miss," he said, his voice barely above a whisper. "Please read it when you're alone."

Before she could respond, he had turned and begun to walk away, his figure soon lost among the villagers. Amelda looked down at the letter in her hand, feeling its unexpected weight.

Returning to her mother's cottage, she climbed the narrow staircase to her childhood room, feeling a curious tension simmering just beneath the surface. Her mother was downstairs, immersed in her daily routines, leaving her with the quiet she needed. Sitting by the window, the daylight casting a soft glow across the wooden floor, she carefully unfolded the letter.

The handwriting was shaky, almost hesitant, though the script was recognisable as that of someone who had once been practised and refined. She read:

Miss Amelda,

I cannot in good conscience remain silent, knowing what I know. The Duke has left Langston Manor, his purpose to travel to the capital for a marriage that he hopes might give him reprieve from his family's curse. But I fear, in his departure, he may find no freedom but rather the grave. I do not know what drives him to pursue this path, nor why he would leave in such a state, but he did not seem himself, not since you parted. In truth, he has not been himself at all. I implore you to return to Langston, for his sake and perhaps your own. There is more at work in these halls than mere gossip, I am afraid.

May you consider carefully, and return safely.

The letter was unsigned.

Amelda read the words over and over, feeling a chill settle over her. Isaac had left for the capital – she had known that would be his next move, but she had hoped the distance might grant him some respite, some chance to regain his balance. Now, however, she understood that his journey was far from that. The phrase find no freedom but rather the grave echoed in her mind, deepening the dread that now took root.

The part about the curse itself, spoken as if the writer knew every detail, reminded her of how Isaac had spoken of his fears, how he dreaded ending up like the previous Duke tormented by the shadows that drove him to madness. Her heart ached, thinking of him alone, burdened by the weight of that legacy, and the lingering fear that he could not break free.

But what could she do? She was merely a servant, bound by her station and the constraints of propriety, unable to offer him anything more than quiet solace and friendship. Returning to Langston Manor meant crossing back into a world she had just left – a world filled with rules and expectations, all of which would keep them apart, forcing her to deny the growing connection she felt towards him.

But the letter seemed a call to action, an unspoken plea that tugged at her heart, urging her to set aside her fears and return. She couldn't ignore the foreboding sense that Isaac needed someone by his side, someone who understood him beyond the expectations of the estate and the weight of his family's name. If he truly believed in the curse – and her brief encounters with the late Duke had suggested it was more than superstition – then she had to do something. She couldn't leave him to face it alone.

With a resolute sigh, she folded the letter carefully and slipped it into her pocket. She would return to Langston Manor.

Chapter Eighteen

Isaac lay still, swathed in thick blankets in the dim light of his room, the heavy curtains drawn against the day outside. The flickering shadows from the bedside candle played tricks on his weary mind, casting dark shapes across the walls that seemed to warp and stretch. Each time he closed his eyes, nightmares clawed at his consciousness, nightmares where the family curse manifested as shadows, ready to swallow him whole.

The memory of his accident still felt fresh, its images branded onto his mind. He could recall every moment – the jarring of the carriage wheels as they met the uneven road, the sudden shudder as it lurched, tipping precariously, and then the sickening sound of wood splintering and metal crunching as the vehicle overturned. That horrific moment when the world spun in chaos, and he'd felt his own helplessness, trapped beneath debris, and the unforgiving cold of the rain, each returning to him night after night. He could still smell the damp earth where he had been pinned, and in the darkest hours, the scent haunted him, a visceral reminder of how close he'd come to the grave.

A cough pulled him from his thoughts, and Isaac blinked as the physician, a young man with a serious face, stood at the foot of his bed, scratching notes onto a small pad. Yes, he'd arrived yesterday, and was going to examine him. That was the last he remembered when he was sure his eyes were open.

"You were fortunate, Your Grace," the physician murmured, glancing up briefly. "By all rights, I would have expected injuries far worse. It's a wonder you managed to get back to Langston at all, and I heard, barked orders for several books from the library on your return – the wonders shall never cease."

Isaac grimaced, trying to sit up, but the soreness in his ribs reminded him to stay still. "What exactly…?" His voice was hoarse, strained from both his physical ordeal and the fitful rest he'd had since.

"Several fractured ribs, extensive bruising, I've had to stitch your shoulder, and a twisted ankle," the physician replied with a neutral expression, though his eyes betrayed a trace of concern. "It seems adrenaline carried you back. And perhaps…something stronger kept you from death's door."

Isaac winced as he shifted, feeling the dull throb of pain with each breath. "You mean luck?"

"Perhaps," the physician replied tactfully, "but regardless, you must rest for a time. Complete bed-rest. Any further strain could worsen the fractures. I'll have one of the servants attend to you as often as needed."

As the physician departed, Isaac sank further into the pillows, feeling the chill of the room seep into his bones and the cloying scent of some ointment that wafted up from under his shirt. The unbidden thought crept into his mind – What if the curse were at work? What if his death was the cost of denying it?

And yet, the curse had never felt like such a tangible threat, not until he'd become aware of his feelings for Amelda, and now with so much evidence that it sought his demise he lacked the sensibility to deny it's existence with his whole being. With the clarity that came from surviving a brush with death, the truth loomed in his mind, undeniable and raw. He loved her, truly, and the real curse he feared now was not a family legacy and untimely death, but rather the looming spectre of living a life that denied that love. He had witnessed much of his father's descent – a life consumed by regret, distrust, and isolation. His parents marriage, haunted by emptiness then death, had only deepened his misery. Isaac had sworn never to follow that path, yet he saw how the shadows of it lay before him, threatening to pull him into the same abyss.

Better to live truly, even if only briefly, than to wither under the weight of his forebears' choices, he thought, as the ache in his chest became something more than physical pain. He could not deny it any longer.

The following days blurred together in a haze of forced bed-rest, pain, and contemplation. Servants came and went, each bringing some small comfort – a warm meal, a fresh jug of water, the occasional whispered query about his health. Williams himself paid several visits, discreet yet attentive, his gaze lingering now and again with a look Isaac could not quite interpret. But despite the routine care, Isaac felt the solitude profoundly. Only one person had the power to dissolve it, yet she was the one he had decided to distance himself from, for the sake of his duty and her safety.

It was early one evening, as the day's light waned into a hazy, purple dusk, that Williams entered with a stack of letters. Isaac sifted through them absently, his hands trembling slightly as he saw the wax seal bearing the royal insignia on one particular envelope. He broke it open, his eyes scanning the missive, each line reinforcing what he already knew the King's counsel would demand: the importance of marriage, the importance of preserving the noble bloodline, and the importance of bringing forth an heir to sustain the Blackwood name.

The familiar sense of duty pressed down on him with a heavy hand, but well and truly, he felt defiant. In the aftermath of his accident, his heart rebelled against these constraints more fiercely than it ever had. He had never dared to ask what he wanted from life, sincerely wanted, nor did he believe it was his right to pursue it. But there was no denying it now. The legacy of his name meant nothing if it brought him to ruin, and the life he faced without Amelda was one in which he could see no joy, only bitter endurance.

When Williams returned to the room, Isaac motioned him to draw closer. "Williams," he began, his voice heavy, "there's something I need you to understand."

The butler nodded, his expression attentive but cautious. "Of course, Your Grace."

Isaac hesitated, his gaze distant. "You were with my father through most of his life, weren't you?"

Williams's expression softened, and he inclined his head. "Indeed, I was, Your Grace. From his birth to his final days."

"You must have seen…" Isaac trailed off, struggling to find the words. "How he was consumed. The curse, the isolation…it changed him."

Williams's gaze held a glint of understanding, though he remained respectfully silent, allowing Isaac to gather his thoughts.

"He…married for duty, didn't he?" Isaac continued, a lump in his throat thickening his voice. "He never found love in his marriage, and it left him…desolate. I'm beginning to fear that by following in his footsteps, I'll meet the same fate."

Williams looked down, his expression unreadable. "Your father believed he was fulfilling his duty, Your Grace. And while he may have been burdened, he was…dedicated despite the distance, even if it brought him little joy."

Isaac closed his eyes, feeling the familiar pressure of that word – duty. It had been the lodestone of his life, the guiding principle instilled in him since childhood. But he saw that duty alone could become a chain, binding him to a life of quiet desperation.

"I cannot be him, Williams," Isaac said softly, his voice laced with both fear and resolve. "If I am to lead this family, to uphold our name…I must do it on my own terms. And I cannot abandon my heart in the process."

Williams studied him, his expression remaining neutral, though Isaac sensed the faintest hint of approval in the man's gaze.

"Your Grace," Williams finally said, "if I may be so bold, you have always shown a strength of will that is…unique. Should you choose to follow your heart, it may yet bring light to Langston, a light we have not seen for many years."

Isaac looked up, a flicker of hope igniting within him. For the first time in days, he felt the weight of his fears ease, replaced by the glimmer of a path forward – one that would require courage, but also one that would be true to himself.

After Williams departed, Isaac lay back against the pillows, exhaustion settling over him. The royal letter still lay open on the bedside table, its formal words fading into irrelevance as he thought instead of Amelda. Her laughter, her strength, her presence that had been his comfort through all of his recent dark days.

His resolve hardened, clear as the steady beat of his heart. He would not live a life of regret and bitterness, nor would he allow the shadows of the past to dictate his future. Whatever the curse might hold, he was willing to face it – not with fear, but with the unwavering truth of his own heart.

In the depths of his dreams that night, there were no nightmares, no shadows. Instead, he dreamt of her – of sunlight and warmth, of a future shaped not by duty alone, but by love.

Isaac reclined against the pillows, a stack of documents resting atop a wooden tray across his lap. Though his ribs ached with each slight movement, he forced himself to concentrate on the estate's affairs, sorting through tenant requests, financial ledgers, and letters from his solicitors. It was a relief, in some small way, to focus on something external – to turn his mind from the maddening weight of his thoughts. And yet, as he read line after line of neatly written script, a sense of inevitability loomed.

Just as he was finishing a letter from the estate's solicitor, a light knock sounded at his door.

"Come in," Isaac called, shifting the tray to his bedside table.

The door creaked open, and one of the household servants entered, carrying a leather-bound journal in his gloved hands. The man was elderly, with a thin frame and the stooped posture of one who had spent decades in service. Though Isaac knew each servant by name – a practice he had adopted to honour the generations of loyalty within the household – he struggled now to recall this man's. He only remembered that his father had been in service before him, and that his family's presence in Langston went back almost as far as the Blackwood line itself.

"Good evening, Your Grace," the man said, his voice steady, though softened with age.

"Good evening," Isaac replied, his eyes drawn to the book in the man's hands. It looked worn, its edges frayed and its binding faded. "What do you have there?"

"A journal, Your Grace," the servant replied, stepping forward and extending it with both hands. "It was discovered in one of the attic chests, quite by accident. Mr Williams thought it might be of…interest to you, given its contents."

Isaac took the journal, curiosity piqued. "Thank you," he said, noting the slight nod of understanding that passed between them. As the servant bowed and retreated from the room, Isaac turned the book over, studying it. There was no title or indication of the author on the outside, but the leather felt old, as if it had borne witness to generations of secrets.

Settling back against his pillows, he opened the journal, and his breath caught as he recognised the scrawling hand of an ancestor – the Blackwood Duke who had originally invoked the curse that haunted his bloodline. His handwriting was as indelible as his own blood, painted into the family crest itself, he'd recognise it in a heartbeat even if his name was not also signed into the ancient pages.

The journal's early pages spoke of ordinary matters: estate records, accounts of tenant disputes, details of harvests and trades. But as Isaac read on, a different narrative emerged – one that was deeply personal, laden with heartbreak, and, he realised, the very origin of the curse that had cast its shadow over his family.

The duke had been young, barely a man when he'd first met her – an alchemist's daughter, a woman of great beauty and wit, and well beneath his station. She had been kind, wise beyond her years, and he had been captivated by her. Though he could have easily married her in secrecy, as many of his contemporaries might have done, he'd dreamt instead of a life openly shared, one built on mutual love rather than duty. His heart had been lost to her, and it was she alone who had made him feel free of the burdens that came with his title. But this love, it seemed, had been doomed from the start.

"How I longed to be a man without obligations," the journal read in a faded, brittle ink. "But my family's blood has demands, and in the end, I could not escape them. I left her, with a heart as heavy as any punishment, and married another. Yet from that moment, I knew I was marked, cursed by my own hand for denying the truth."

Isaac's hands trembled as he turned the pages, the duke's regret sinking deeper with each entry. The man had gone on to marry a noblewoman from an influential family, their union solidifying the family's young position in Briarvale and securing its fortune. But his true love had not accepted her fate so readily. In her despair and anger, she had called upon powers Isaac's ancestor had dismissed as mere superstition. She had cursed him and his lineage, he'd written the words as if she spoke them onto the page "May the Blackwood line forever know the pain etched in my heart".

In the days following the curse, the duke's marriage had quickly turned bitter. His wife had borne him children, but their union grew cold and distant. Each year, the sense of discontent and anguish only deepened, until he was finally consumed by it, living out his final days in dark isolation. The journal ended with a simple, haunting line: "This is the fate I've brought upon my scions and theirs, should they make the same choice."

Isaac's chest tightened as he closed the journal, his mind reeling. The implications of what he'd read weighed heavily on him. His father's life had been marked by an unspoken sorrow that Isaac now understood all too clearly. His parents' marriage had been one of duty, a hollow partnership that had festered into resentment and left his father a solitary figure, plagued by the curse until his death.

This is my choice now, he realised, the thought filling him with both dread and clarity. If he continued down the path of duty, choosing a marriage purely to fulfil the expectations of his title, he would condemn himself to the same fate. The same misery, the same dark, haunted existence. And he knew, with a certainty that terrified him, that denying his heart would be to deny the very essence of himself.

As the night deepened, Isaac lay in bed, his mind drifting to Amelda. He thought of her footsteps along the corridors, how he came to hope for their familiar pattern while he worked, her radiant smile, the way she saw him not as a Duke but simply as a man. The connection they shared had been his refuge in ways he hadn't fully comprehended until now. It was love – love he had been too afraid to name, too fearful of what it might mean for both of them.

But if he ignored that love, if he married another simply to adhere to his duties as a noble of Briarvale, he knew what awaited him. A lifetime of emptiness, a heart heavy with regret, and a mind that would bring him no peace. The curse was not merely superstition; it was the living proof of what his choices could cost him. It was a prophecy he was not going to fulfil, as real as magic and as sure as night following the day that whether the curse was supernatural or of his own mind, the fruits would be the same if he wavered in his conviction.

In that quiet moment, the decision crystallised in his mind, clearer than ever before. He would not follow the same path as his father, nor would he allow duty to become his prison.

If he was to be the Duke of Blackwood, he would do so on his own terms, with a heart unbound by fear or obligation.

He would choose love, even if it meant defying every expectation placed upon him.

Chapter Nineteen

The early morning mist clung to the trees lining the estate's path as Amelda approached the towering gates of Langston. The estate loomed above her, familiar yet somehow colder than she remembered. Since the day she had left, every footstep away from this place had felt like a weight lifting from her chest, a distance that would afford her the freedom to bury whatever had taken root between herself and Isaac. Yet the letter – unsigned, mysterious, and laden with an unspoken importance – had drawn her back. Now, each step felt much the same, a burden dropping from her shoulders as sure as the weight of her dark green travelling cloak.

Upon hearing of his accident, the news blazing into her village, the world around her had turned hollow, an unending echo of horror that threatened to fill every silent moment. The Duke had nearly died. Isaac had nearly died. It was a thought too painful to bear, and her heart ached with the knowledge that she had never truly left him behind at all.

Entering the manor, Amelda sensed a muted stillness in the air, as if the entire household had fallen into a wary hush since the accident. Williams, appearing at the base of the staircase, met her with a solemn nod. His expression was sombre, lacking the usual knowing glance he often gave her, replaced instead by a shadow of concern.

"How is he?" she asked, the words nearly a whisper.

"His Grace is recovering," Williams replied, his voice low. "The physician has advised bed-rest, and he is rarely without pain. I'll take you to him." She did not ask him why she was allowed to visit the Duke, nor did she want to know how the elder servant knew she wanted to see him.

Amelda followed Williams up the familiar staircase and through the winding corridors that led to Isaac's chambers, heart pounding as each step brought her closer. She knew she had no right to feel this deeply, to care so fiercely, and yet each nerve in her body thrummed with an urgency that was almost unbearable. In the days she had spent away, she had attempted to deny her attachment to him, to remind herself of the barriers between them. But the thought of him lying somewhere alone, suffering, drove any self-preserving sense from her mind.

When they reached Isaac's door, Williams nodded again before quietly slipping away. Amelda stood at the threshold, staring at the heavy oak, and took a steadying breath before pushing it open.

The room was dim, save for a sliver of sunlight piercing the drawn curtains and the glow of barely lit embers in the hearth. Isaac lay in his bed, his head resting against the pillows and his face shadowed in half-light. His chest rose and fell with a deep but uneasy rhythm, his brow faintly creased even in sleep. She could see the bandages peeking out beneath his nightshirt, binding the injuries from his carriage accident, and it was clear that even unconscious, he bore the marks of pain.

Steeling herself, Amelda moved forward, each step careful, lest she disturb him. She reached the edge of his bed and hesitated, gazing down at him as if the weight of her sorrow might be communicated in silence. His face, drawn and pale, looked older than she remembered; gone was the light-hearted glance she'd often seen when he smiled at her. It was a jarring reminder of the curse that had plagued his family for generations, a shadow was now claiming its hold over him.

In the stillness, her own guilt welled up, suffusing her mind until it became too much to bear. How had she let things come to this? How could she have let herself linger here at the manor, all but pretending she could fit into Isaac's life, when she had known all along that her place was far outside the walls of his world? She knew now that she had been selfish, even if unknowingly so.

She leaned closer, her hand hovering just above his, though she dared not touch it. Her voice, when she spoke, was barely a murmur, soft and tremulous in the quiet of the room.

"I'm so sorry, Isaac," she whispered, her eyes stinging. "I read a journal in the library – written by the first Duke of Blackwood. I know what it means for you, what it demands of you."

She paused, her words catching in her throat. It felt strange, almost improper, to speak so freely, yet the words tumbled out as if years of silence had pressed them forward. He would never know of this confession, and yet she found herself unburdening her heart as if he might somehow understand, even in slumber.

"When I read about your ancestor… about how he chose duty over his heart…" she continued, swallowing hard. "It's the same path you're expected to take, isn't it? To follow what is expected rather than what you truly want. And I know of the price the curse demands too. To make a choice fresh faced in love. And I – I fear I have been a hindrance to you, Isaac, making the union of duty and love nigh impossible for you. I let myself linger here, thinking I was merely your friend, that I could keep my heart in check. But I was wrong."

She brushed a trembling hand across her cheek, a tear slipping free as she continued, her gaze never leaving his face even as the tears in her eyes turned the outline of him into watery blurs.

"Perhaps I was foolish, allowing myself to get this close. I see now how selfish I've been. If there's even the slightest chance that you could find someone – a true love, someone worthy and suitable – who could break this curse, then I must let you go. I should." Her voice dropped to a broken whisper. "Because whatever I feel… it isn't enough. Not for you. Not for the curse that looms over your family."

The words hung in the air, as fragile as glass, and yet they had a weight all their own. She understood now that their connection, whatever it was, could never transcend the reality of his world. She was a servant, nothing more, and to pretend otherwise would only lead them both to ruin. It had always been a childish dream, one she should never have allowed herself to entertain.

Her heart clenched, and she closed her eyes, trying to steady herself.

"Perhaps this is the punishment the curse has for you," she said softly, almost to herself. "To love someone you can never be with… and for me, to care for you as I do, and know it can never be."

Amelda forced herself to step back, though her gaze lingered on his face, memorising the lines of it, the contours softened by sleep. A part of her ached with the desire to reach out, to brush a hand across his brow or murmur words of comfort. But she knew she couldn't. She had no place here, no right to offer solace.

In silence, she watched him for a moment longer before turning away, feeling the sting of tears that would fall if she remained any longer.

Amelda had nearly reached the door when she heard a faint stir from behind her, the softest murmur of her name.

"Amelda?"

Her heart jolted as she turned. Isaac's eyes were open, though unfocused, fixed upon her as if she were some spectre that had appeared only in his fevered mind. He looked at her with a pained curiosity, his voice barely a rasp.

"Is it really you, or am I dreaming again?" he asked, his tone raw and bewildered, as though he were afraid to hear her answer.

Amelda took a hesitant step forward, her resolve wavering. She wanted to leave, to spare them both the heartache of another impossible moment. But there was something in his eyes – a yearning, a desperation that broke through her carefully guarded distance.

She cleared her throat softly and wiped under her eyes. "It's me, Your Grace," she whispered. "I'm here."

For a moment, he looked almost disappointed, his expression wavering between longing and resignation. "Am I cursed even in dreams?" he muttered to himself, a bitter note in his voice. "To be haunted by that which I cannot hold?"

"Isaac," she breathed, more to herself than him. She took another step forward, her body drawn by something she couldn't quite name, her own heart beating painfully against her ribs.

He closed his eyes briefly, as if the sound of his name from her lips brought him some fleeting relief. When he opened them again, there was a new glint of clarity, his gaze softening even as it seemed to grow more intense. "If you're here… if you're really here," he murmured, "come closer, Amelda. Let me… let me see you."

She knew she should resist, to keep the boundary between them, but some force stronger than reason drew her forward. She found herself moving toward him until she was at his side, close enough to feel the faint warmth of his breath and to see the flecks of gold in his grey eyes as they lingered on her face.

Isaac's hand lifted from the bed, unsteady and tentative. He reached out, and though she knew it would be wise to step back, to deny him even this comfort, she couldn't bring herself to move. Slowly, his fingers found hers, his touch feather-light and uncertain. He let out a long, shuddering breath, as though the contact had eased something deep within him.

"You're real," he whispered, his voice barely audible. "Amelda, I… I thought you'd gone. I expected a resignation letter with every day you'd not returned."

She nodded, unable to bring words to her own lips as his fingers entwined with hers. He gazed at her, his expression shifting, as though he were coming to a decision he had been putting off for too long.

"I cannot pretend any longer," he said, his voice rough but resolute. "For months, I've battled against this, against what I feel for you. I've tried to convince myself it's wrong, that it's a weakness, a danger to us both. And yet… every time I see you, every time you enter a room, it is as if nothing else matters."

Amelda looked down, her fingers tightening involuntarily in his grasp. "Isaac… you mustn't say this," she whispered, though even to her own ears, the words sounded hollow.

"But it's the truth," he said, his voice gaining strength, his gaze unwavering. "Amelda, my heart has been bound to you from the moment we met, even if I lacked the courage to admit it, even when I dared probe for some mutual affection from you and was denied. And the curse… the curse has only tormented me because I have tried to deny what is true as well. I know that now."

She swallowed hard, the weight of his words pressing down upon her. Every instinct told her to pull away, to protect him from the pain their impossible love would bring. And yet, her heart ached with the knowledge that she too could not pretend any longer.

"This isn't just about the curse," she managed, her voice quivering. "It's about duty, about everything you've been raised to believe. You have a life beyond me, Isaac. A world that expects – demands – certain things from you."

Isaac shook his head, a defiance sparking in his weary eyes. "I refuse to be shackled by duty if it means living a life devoid of what matters most. My family's curse was not the result of mere obligation but of denying their hearts, of choosing a path that led him to darkness. And I... I will not make the same mistake."

He shifted, attempting to sit up, and she instinctively reached forward to steady him. Her hands found his shoulders, and he leaned into her touch, his face inches from hers. The air between them grew thick with unspoken words, the truth they had both fought so hard to avoid now hanging openly between them.

"Amelda," he said, his tone softening, his gaze intense. "Do you not feel it too? This bond between us, stronger than title or station... stronger even than the fear of this curse?"

Her heart pounded in her chest as she met his gaze, every thought of protest fading in the warmth of his eyes. "I... I do," she admitted, the words tumbling out before she could stop them. "But that doesn't make it any easier."

He lifted a hand to her cheek, his touch tender and trembling. "I would rather face the wrath of every curse, the condemnation of society, than live a life without you."

A tear slipped down her cheek as his thumb brushed it away. "What future could we have?" she asked, her voice barely a whisper.

"We will find a way," he replied, his voice filled with quiet but fiery determination. "If love is truly the answer to breaking this curse, then I know no other path than the one that leads to you."

She wanted to argue, to list every reason why this was impossible, but the conviction in his voice melted every objection. In that moment, she realised that he was right – his life had been haunted by shadows, by the legacy of a family cursed by hearts untrue. Yet here, in this small room, there was a glimmer of hope, a chance for something pure to break the chains that bound him.

"I love you, Amelda," he whispered, his lips brushing against her forehead. "And I will not let duty, fear, or even fate itself keep us apart."

She closed her eyes, letting his words wash over her, feeling the depth of his devotion in every syllable. And for the first time, she allowed herself to believe in the possibility of a future, one where love could transcend even the darkest curse. She raised her face to meet his and tentatively leaned into his soft lips, the harshness of his stubble from days in bed meant nothing compared to the insistent way he returned the kiss. Her heart might have leapt from her throat as he gently cradled her jaw and pushed himself against his injuries to sit proper so that he could deepen the kiss further.

Chapter Twenty

The days grew colder as autumn began to slip into winter, but Langston Manor, long plagued by dampness and a weighty sense of dread, felt different somehow. The once unyielding chill and mists seemed to lessen with each passing day, and the oppressive shadow that had clung to the estate appeared to retreat as though it were being pushed back by some invisible hand.

Isaac noticed it first in the smallest of things. The hallways that had felt so dark, even in summer's height, were suddenly filled with soft, warming light as the thin rays of sun pierced through gaps in the clouds, illuminating dust motes as they drifted peacefully through the air. He'd begun to take these small signs as evidence of something far greater: the slow but certain loosening of the curse's grip over the estate.

On a particularly crisp morning, he found himself pausing at a window overlooking the gardens. Once tangled and choked by weeds despite constant management, the grounds had gradually taken on a more welcoming shape since the summer. Now, even as the branches grew bare, the garden seemed peaceful rather than haunted. The paths winding through it were free of the damp, decaying leaves that had always littered the grounds and seemed to shimmer with a vitality he could scarcely remember seeing before.

He thought of Amelda, of her smile when he'd last seen her that very morning in the kitchen while she helped the maids with the linen. Her laugh, soft as a breeze through the trees, had filled him with an undeniable warmth. His love for her, still fresh yet unbreakable, brought him a comfort he hadn't known he could feel in the halls of Langston Manor. It was as if, through his choice to embrace the love between them, something greater than either of them was being set right.

As the servants went about their work, they too began to remark upon the changes. Williams, who had been with the family through near every twist of the curse's many decades, would pause at moments to glance at Isaac with a knowing, almost fatherly pride. The head gardener, a stoic man who rarely commented on anything unrelated to his plants, remarked that the earth itself felt different, almost as though it were breathing easier. Even Cropp seemed to remark at a calm in the woods as he felled the rotted trees that had been marked for removal back in the summer.

The other servants muttered amongst themselves, their voices barely above whispers but filled with wonder.

"Do you feel it too?" asked one maid as she gathered wood for the fires. "The manor doesn't feel as heavy any more. I went into the east wing and didn't even flinch once!"

"I do," replied her friend, folding linen with practised hands. "It's as if the ghost there was banished. I used to dread going into the east wing too! Now, it just feels… normal, as it should."

Meanwhile, Isaac busied himself with overseeing affairs on the estate, spending his days meeting with tenants, ensuring that their needs would be met as winter approached. He walked the fields with the farmers once the physician cleared him, exchanging advice and hearing of their plans for the next season. For years, his father had kept such matters at arm's length, only stepping in when it became necessary. But Isaac took comfort in these interactions; he felt connected to his lands and his people for the first time, as if by caring for them, he was helping to break whatever dark thread had bound his family to a life of isolation and sorrow.

The accidents, too, had ceased. There were no more falling branches or precarious statues ready to topple. The servants, once fearful of every shadow and creak in the walls, moved through the halls with a renewed sense of ease – and he noted, that they not longer moved about unseen. Isaac couldn't ignore the pattern – the timing of it all was too perfect, too coincidental. It was as though his decision to follow his heart, his love for Amelda, had set something right, like a key finally turning in a lock.

Despite the practical demands of his position, his mind often wandered to thoughts of Amelda. She was often out of sight, tending to her duties with care, but he'd catch glimpses of her at times – walking through the corridor with an armful of linen or talking softly with the other servants. And though their connection remained unspoken in public, there was a gentle smile she reserved just for him, one that warmed him as much as a roaring fire.

One afternoon, Isaac found himself in the library, surrounded by tomes that had once felt like relics of a darker past. He pulled down an old book of poetry, one of his mother's favourites, remembering her voice as she read to him when he was a child. She had long been gone, her memory overshadowed by his father's grim influence, but in that quiet, sunlit room, he felt closer to her. It was as if the love he held in his heart now was mending more than just the curse – it was bringing pieces of his own family history back into the light.

Just then, Williams entered, carrying a tray with tea and a few slices of buttered bread.

"Thought you might like a bit of refreshment, Your Grace," he said, setting the tray on a nearby table. His expression was carefully composed, though there was a faint glint of satisfaction in his eyes.

"Thank you, Williams." Isaac gave the butler an appreciative smile. "I've been noticing some… changes around the estate. It's as though a cloud has parted and finally let the sun in."

Williams nodded, pouring tea into a delicate porcelain cup. "Many have observed it, Your Grace. The staff have remarked upon the lightness in the air. Even the ground seems different somehow." The butler was privy to much of what happened within the walls, though neither of them spoke openly on what exactly had transpired.

Isaac took a sip, the warm liquid soothing him as he looked out of the library windows at the grounds stretching into the horizon. "I never quite realised the toll the curse had taken. It's as if my family's grief, its pain, settled in these walls, in the very stones of Langston Manor."

Williams hesitated before speaking, his voice gentle but filled with conviction. "Sometimes, all that is needed to heal old wounds is for someone to choose a different path, to be brave enough to defy the patterns set by those before him."

Isaac absorbed this, nodding thoughtfully. He did not say outright what he knew, but he alluded it to it well enough. "I never wanted this curse to define my life. And yet... I cannot deny it has shaped so much of who I am."

The butler cleared his throat. "Then perhaps, Your Grace, it is time to allow yourself the freedom to create a life beyond the curse wholly. It seems... it seems to me that you are already well on that path."

A warmth filled Isaac's chest, a new sense of hope blooming within him. For so long, he had been shackled by a duty he barely understood, by fears instilled by his father's mistakes and the weight of his family's suffering. Now, for the first time, he saw a future in which he could be both dutiful and true to himself.

As he looked out over the grounds, a gentle snow began to fall, the first of the season. The light dusting softened the landscape, blanketing it in pristine white. Isaac felt as though he were witnessing not just the turning of the seasons but the start of something new, a rebirth of sorts for Langston.

The days that followed were filled with more small, almost imperceptible changes. Rooms that had long been shut were opened, and furniture covered in dust sheets was brought back into use. Even the air felt different, fresher, as though each gust of wind that swept through the halls carried away another layer of gloom. The servants whispered that it was as if the manor itself were waking from a long slumber.

Each time he saw Amelda, her presence seemed to renew his sense of purpose. Though they kept a respectful distance in front of others, there was a silent understanding, a bond between them that transcended the need for words. And as he watched her go about her duties, a quiet contentment settled over him. He was beginning to realise that his choice to pursue happiness, to let love into his life, was the very thing that had begun to loosen the curse's hold.

Isaac's mother had once told him stories of how the land reflected the heart of its steward, he remembered her reading to him now, as a small boy. The Blackwood family had long been plagued by sorrow and bitterness, and the estate had mirrored that darkness. But now, with love in his heart, he could see how the curse was retreating, like a shadow fleeing the dawn.

As winter took hold, Langston Manor continued its transformation, revealing a side of itself that few had ever seen. The warmth that Isaac felt within himself seemed to echo through the very walls, filling the manor with a sense of hope he'd never thought possible. He had made his choice, and in doing so, he had set a new course not only for himself but for the Blackwood family as a whole.

With each passing day, Isaac grew more certain of one thing: he had been right to choose love. For in choosing it, he had unlocked a strength he hadn't known he possessed –

a strength that was now freeing his family from the shadows that had haunted them for generations.

It was a quiet evening, the last warmth of autumn fading into the crisp air of winter. Isaac had taken Amelda for a walk in the grounds, his heart racing, hidden under the calm poise he maintained in her presence. The paths they walked were familiar, each step laden with memories of their shared moments, from soft-spoken confidences to the subtle glances that had long since revealed more than words ever could. When they reached a clearing by the old oak tree, Isaac stopped, turning to face her, the light of the dying sun casting a golden glow across her face. She looked at him, slightly puzzled, and he hesitated, words caught in his throat as he held her gaze.

"Amelda," he began, his voice unsteady but resolute. "I spent too many days and nights trying to convince myself that the way I felt for you is something I could deny... and since I realised I could not, it as if I have never felt more right in myself. I have come to see that without you, this estate, my life, every title, every duty, it all feels insignificant." He drew a deep breath, taking her hands in his, the warmth of her fingers grounding him as he knelt, never taking his eyes from hers. "I don't wish for a life where I must pretend. Not any more. Marry me, Amelda. Let us defy the expectations together. I ask for nothing but a life that we can build, with our own hands, on our own terms."

For a moment, she was speechless, eyes wide and brimming with emotion. The world around them seemed to hold its breath, the gentle rustling of leaves their only witness. Amelda's voice was barely above a whisper as she replied, "Isaac... are you certain? You know what this means, what it will cost." He nodded, his gaze steadfast, filled with a certainty that left no room for doubt. He'd abstain the title to Theodore if pressed. A smile broke over her face as she gently pulled him to his feet, her arms finding their way around him as she whispered her answer, her voice steady and filled with quiet joy. "Yes, Isaac. I would go nowhere else, if I could be here, with you."

The morning of the wedding dawned with a tender, silvery light glimmering through the frosty windows of Langston Manor. The world outside lay quiet and crisp, bathed in a winter stillness that gave the air a sense of reverence. There were no crowds of nobility, no pomp or ceremony, only the few who mattered most in Isaac and Amelda's lives, gathered together in one of the estate's parlours. The servants had first been filled with equal parts delight and excitement when he'd asked for the room to be prepared, especially as now they knew of his intended bride. There was trepidation of course, that followed, given the uncertainty that would follow his choice – but Isaac assured them that even if forced to step down from his title, Langston would find him a loyal tenant under the new stewardship of his cousin. It abated some concerns, and their excitement assuaged the less certain.

The room itself had been prepared simply. Ivy, holly, and a few evergreen branches were arranged around the mantelpiece, their dark leaves and bright red berries a subtle nod to the season. A single tall candle, lit in the early hours, glowed from the windowsill, casting a soft amber light over the intimate setting.

Isaac stood beside his solicitor, his usually steady composure softened by an unmistakable air of anticipation. He wore a tailored, dark coat with a cravat of forest green silk – a subtle but thoughtful touch, chosen in memory of the same shade Amelda had worn when she'd returned to the estate, been there at his bedside. As he waited, a warmth spread through him that belied the icy chill outside, filling him with a rare, unguarded excitement.

Williams stood at his other side, looking more like a proud father than a servant, his usually stoic expression softened with a quiet, contented smile. He'd watched over the young Duke since he was a child, and it was clear to him now that this was the day Isaac had truly stepped into the life he was meant for.

Across from them, Amelda's family gathered – her mother, a petite woman with lines of both age and laughter etched across her face. She was stood beside Amelda's elder sister, Mary who was starting to fill out expectantly, and her husband, Nelson. Her younger brother Edwin hovered close by, looking both shy and excited in his best suit.

While the rest of the staff had been told not to crowd the parlour, he knew many were in the halls outside and would crane their ears to the door after Amelda stepped in.

The door opened, and in walked Amelda. Her dress was simple yet lovely, a light cream muslin, slightly gathered at the bust and trimmed with a modest lace at the cuffs and neckline. She had gathered her hair back, leaving a few loose dark red curls around her face that framed her features softly, and she held a small bouquet of winter flowers, tied together with a ribbon of deep green. She stepped forward, her gaze meeting Isaac's, and in that moment, it was as if the entire room held its breath.

As she joined him, Isaac reached for her hand, feeling the warmth of her fingers in his own. Their eyes met, and the world around them seemed to fade, leaving only the two of them standing side by side, hearts beating as one. In their silence, a thousand thoughts passed between them – words unsaid, promises unspoken, all wrapped in the shared knowledge that they were on the verge of a life that neither of them had dared hope for.

The ceremony was conducted by Isaac's solicitor, he brokered no judgement on the decision, and he read the words of the service with an air of solemnity that suited the quiet joy of the occasion. He spoke of commitment, of trust, and of the strength it would take to walk through life together, hand in hand.

As he recited the vows, Isaac's voice was steady but filled with emotion, his gaze fixed solely on Amelda. "I, Isaac

Blackwood, take you, Amelda Gedge, to be my wedded wife. To love and to cherish, from this day forward, for better, for worse, for richer, for poorer, in sickness and in health… for all the days of my life." His hand tightened gently around hers, his eyes shining with every ounce of affection in his soul.

Amelda's voice, soft and unwavering, carried a warmth that filled the room as she repeated the vows, her words like a promise stitched into the very air between them. "I, Amelda Gedge, take you, Isaac Blackwood, to be my wedded husband. To love and to cherish, from this day forward, for better, for worse, for richer, for poorer, in sickness and in health… for all the days of my life."

When the vows were complete, Isaac's solicitor pronounced them husband and wife, his voice thick with the shared understanding of what this union meant for them both.

And then, at last, Isaac and Amelda turned to one another, and he cupped her face in his hands, his touch gentle and reverent. She leaned into his touch, feeling the warmth of his hands against her cool cheeks, her heart beating as if it might burst from her chest.

As he bent his head towards her, his eyes searched hers, and in that moment, everything – the curse, the world's expectations, the weight of their separate stations – faded away, leaving only the two of them in the quiet sanctuary of each other's presence. He closed the distance between them, his lips meeting hers in a kiss that was both tender and fierce, as though he were pouring his very soul into the embrace.

The kiss deepened, his hands slipping from her face to her waist, drawing her close. Amelda responded, her arms winding around his neck as if to hold him close enough to banish every shadow they'd once known. The warmth of his mouth, the strength in his embrace, made her feel as though she were tethered to him, to the life they would share – a life built on love, a life free from fear.

They drew apart, both breathless, and the room – silent with reverence for the vows they had exchanged – filled with quiet smiles and contented sighs from those closest to them. He even swore he heard a squeak of happiness from outside the door that lead to a wave of fevered whispers. Isaac looked down at Amelda, his heart swelling with a joy he hadn't known was possible, a joy that seemed to spill out from him, infusing every corner of the room.

And as they turned to face the small gathering of their family, hand in hand, Isaac felt that for the first time, he was exactly where he was meant to be. Together, they stepped forward, no longer bound by the chains of their pasts, but ready to embrace a future shaped by the love they had chosen – a future that would be, above all else, theirs.

Chapter Twenty-One

The first soft light of spring crept over Langston Estate, casting a warm glow over the ancient stone walls that had, for centuries, borne witness to generations of Blackwoods and the weight of their burdens. Now, under the clear morning sky, the manor seemed almost reborn, no longer shadowed by the foreboding gloom that had once seeped into its very bones. It was a transformation as real as the light breaking across the countryside, and it felt, to Isaac and Amelda, as though Langston itself had drawn a breath of relief.

In the months since their wedding, life had taken on a rhythm filled with the hopeful work of building anew, the repairs in the east wing had begun as soon as the frost of winter had broken, and letters had poured in each day bringing their shock, congratulations, and in some cases, dismay that he'd not once thought of their daughters. Amelda moved through the manor each morning with a sense of purpose, her presence bringing warmth to spaces long left untouched and uncared for. It was a transition for her, from servant to lady of the manor, but one she had fallen neatly into.

Together, she and Isaac restored rooms that had lain dormant, filling them with vibrant new life, colours, and furnishings chosen for comfort rather than formality. Langston was becoming a home, not only to them but to the entire household. Even the servants, who had once murmured of ill-fortune and curse-laden halls, seemed uplifted by the changes, their tasks taken on with greater ease, and a sense of belonging filling every corner of the estate.

Isaac, too, felt the freedom in this renewal, his days filled with plans for the land, improvements to the tenant farms, and the quiet satisfaction of turning his vision into something tangible. There hadn't been news yet that he'd have to leave his title to his cousin, even Theodore had sent his regards to them both for all the joy they could muster together. The echoes of duty, legacy, and titles seemed to fade each day, replaced by the knowledge that he was forging a legacy of his own making, one built upon love and choice rather than obligation. In Amelda, he had found his truest companion, a partner who understood the weight of his past and the bright potential of their future. They moved side by side through the tasks of the day, and each night, as they shared quiet moments, the simple closeness they had fought so hard to attain filled him with a gratitude he could scarcely put into words.

Clara stood just inside the door to Amelda's new sitting room, hands clasped nervously in front of her apron, gaze cast to the floor. Despite having spent years working alongside Amelda, the newly minted Lady Blackwood, Clara now found herself hesitating, as though a great gulf lay between them that she was unsure how to cross. She had brought tea and fresh flowers, but now, in the quiet of the morning, her feet were rooted to the spot, weighed down by a notion that her friend was now impossibly far above her.

"Clara," Amelda's voice was warm as she looked up from her writing desk, "I'd hoped you'd come by."

"Thank you, m'lady," Clara answered, the unfamiliar title slipping awkwardly from her mouth. She kept her gaze fixed on her hands, cheeks colouring. "I didn't want to disturb you, with you being... as you are now."

Amelda let out a soft, gentle laugh and crossed the room to where Clara stood. "As I am now?" she repeated, resting a hand on Clara's shoulder. "Clara, it's just me – Amelda, or Melly as I allowed you to call me before. I may have married Isaac, but I haven't changed. I'm the same person I was when we used to share tea in the kitchens and gossip about the late Duke's strange habits. Nothing's different, truly."

Clara's eyes flickered upward briefly, still uncertain. "But you're Lady Blackwood now. It wouldn't be proper of me to… well, to think of you the same way as before."

"But that's exactly what I want," Amelda replied, a touch of earnestness in her voice. "I don't want you to call me 'Lady Blackwood' or feel like you need to keep your distance. To me, you're still my friend, Clara, just as you've always been. Please, don't feel as though you have to behave differently. I'd be heartbroken to lose your friendship over a title."

After a moment's hesitation, Clara let herself smile, relief mingling with fondness. "If you're sure, Melly," she murmured, slipping back to the familiar nickname. "I was so afraid things would be… well, that they'd have to be different now."

"They don't," Amelda assured her, giving her friend's shoulder a gentle squeeze. "If there's one thing I can promise, Clara, it's that you can always be yourself with me. No airs, no graces. Just us."

"But I can't ask you to help me fold the big linens any more." Clara's smile widened as she nodded, the last of her reservations melting away.

"Once in a blue moon. I might come to miss the laundry." Amelda winked. And just like that, they both knew that no matter how the estate changed, or how life shifted, their friendship would remain untouched.

The arrival of spring marked a new era for Langston Estate, bringing with it not only a bloom of wildflowers along the estate grounds but also the promise of acceptance that neither Isaac nor Amelda could have foreseen. News of their union had travelled far and wide, eventually reaching the ears of King Henry himself. While Isaac had anticipated the King's interest, he had not expected a personal visit; so, when word arrived that His Majesty's carriage would soon be seen on the long path to Langston once the early spring flooding on the roads cleared, the household stirred with anticipation and just a touch of anxiety.

By the time the King's entourage approached the estate, Langston was looking its finest. Lush greenery, the likes of which hadn't been seen for decades, filled the grounds, and the sun cast a warm, even light across the manor, its stone façade no longer weighed down by shadows. As the carriages rolled into view, Isaac and Amelda stood side by side in front of the grand entrance, their hands clasped discreetly, prepared to greet their sovereign with every bit of the respect his title commanded.

The King stepped out of his carriage with a measured grace, his expression one of careful observation as he took in the estate before him. Though his gaze held a flicker of reserve, it softened as he beheld the transformation that had overtaken Langston. The once-foreboding manor now exuded a warm, lively charm, and his discerning eyes took in every detail, from the lush gardens to the brightened stone walls.

"Your Majesty," Isaac greeted him with a respectful bow, his voice steady. "Welcome to Langston."

Amelda curtsied, offering the King a warm, open smile. "It is an honour to have you here, Your Majesty."

King Henry inclined his head, his sharp gaze briefly meeting Amelda's. He gave her a slight smile in return, his expression softening further. "Lady Blackwood," he addressed her formally, before turning to Isaac. "And Duke Blackwood, it seems congratulations are in order. News of your marriage reached me in Acicularia, and I must confess, I was… curious."

Isaac kept his composure, even as he felt the weight of his King's scrutiny. "Thank you, Your Majesty," he replied. "I assure you that though my choice was unconventional, it was made with conviction."

The King cast a thoughtful glance around him, his gaze resting on the estate grounds and the manor itself, both undeniably brighter, almost thriving under Amelda's presence. "Indeed," he murmured. "The estate appears to be much transformed since the last I visited under your father." His tone was approving, though a hint of amusement crept in. "It appears that this new Lady Blackwood has worked wonders on both you and your legacy."

Isaac's grip on Amelda's hand tightened slightly, a small smile forming on his lips. "She has done more for me and Langston than words could express, Your Majesty. I cannot imagine a worthier companion."

King Henry turned to Amelda, nodding slightly, acknowledging the courage it had taken to step into such a role. "Then it seems, Lady Blackwood," he said, his tone bearing a hint of admiration, "you are certainly noble enough to have broken the curse over the Blackwood blood." He offered her a slight, genuine bow of respect, acknowledging her place in a way she had never expected from a King.

Amelda's eyes shone, her heart swelling with pride, and she inclined her head graciously, accepting his praise with humility.

As the King continued his tour of the estate, Isaac and Amelda followed, their hearts lightened by his words. They exchanged a glance, each filled with gratitude and a shared, unspoken understanding: they had, together, changed not only the fate of Langston but the course of the Blackwood family itself.

And as the King departed later that afternoon, he left behind not only his blessing but a newfound recognition of the power of love – transformative and liberating, capable of bending the very fabric of history itself.

The story of Langston Estate, once haunted by shadows and curses, had now, at last, come to a close. The weight of the Blackwood legacy lifted, its dark past now fully behind them, Isaac and Amelda embraced a future defined not by duty alone, but by the courage to love. Together, they began a life of promise, looking forward to the days and years that stretched ahead, free and filled with light.

The End

Printed in Great Britain
by Amazon